Just Another Morning

E. Alan Fleischauer

FIRST EDITION JUNE 2020

Copyright 2020 by E. Alan Fleischauer

Kisses for Valentine's

Brett Ulysses Becker, nicknamed "Bub," was finishing his final day at the Hershey plant that produced chocolate kisses after working there for nearly fifty years.

And he was *not* looking forward to retirement.

But he needed to retire. Sarah, his wife of 35 years, was ill, very ill, and she needed constant attention. And there was no one left to take care of her but Brett. Although he was reluctant to do this, he was going to begin his social security at 62 in an attempt to replace his salary. His brother, a financial advisor, had cautioned him not to, telling him to let it ride and grow incrementally until he was 70.

But it wasn't *his* wife who was sick.

So today was his last day. He was the final inspector of the aluminum-wrapped chocolates. Silver, red, and green passed by him at a steady pace. His job was to spot any candy that needed to be removed, and today, to this point, he hadn't seen any. Brett chuckled to himself, thinking that perhaps this was because it was Valentine's Day. Maybe the chocolate gods were looking out for the tasty treats.

Or not.

Since it was his last day, he was doing something that he'd always wanted to do, but had never had the gumption. Occasionally, he would reach out and pick up a kiss, give it a big wet kiss of his own, then throw it back into the flow of colors. Red was his favorite target. He had done that with about half a dozen chocolates and, as he tossed each back onto the conveyor belt, he paused and said a prayer that whoever consumed the kiss would have good luck.

At least, that's what he hoped for.

When the quitting time bell rang, Brett reached for one last kiss. This time, it was a silver one. He gave it a wet smack and was about to throw it back when he thought, *What the hell?*

He tucked the kiss into his shirt pocket.

This last one was for Sarah.

He removed his smock, got in line to punch out, and then headed out to the parking lot, accepting congratulations from some of the longer-term workers who knew it was his last day. He had gotten a nice watch the week before from the company at a small retirement party, as well as a nice bonus that would certainly help with Sarah's medical bills for a month or two.

And so Brett Ulysses Becker, nicknamed Bub, started his rusty 11-year-old Camry, then saluted the ancient brick building and drove out of the parking lot for the last time, with a tearful sigh.

Brett glanced at his dashboard and noticed that his gas gauge showed that he was nearly empty. Inhaling wearily, he pulled into a familiar gas station and filled up with just a few gallons. He pushed his way through the glass door and stood in line behind a middle-aged woman who was wider than she was tall. She had a single-minded look on her face and was buying all sorts of lottery tickets, at least two of each.

Brett waited patiently.

The broad woman finished, sorted through the scratch tickets, and quickly stuffed them into her purse. She paid for them and her gas and left with a determined expression.

Brett moved up as Sahem, the manager, greeted him. "Hey, Bub, I guess it's your last day of work. I bet you're going to miss eating chocolate all day!"

Bub smiled at the familiar joke for the last time. Putting three dollars on the counter, he noticed that the woman had left a scratch ticket behind. Brett picked it up and ran to the door, but her car was halfway down the block.

So he turned back to Sahem and started to give him the ticket.

Sahem backed away as if it were on fire.

"Oh no, I can't take that! It's been paid for, and my faith won't allow me to even think about gambling. Heck, I could be banished if they found out I even touched these scratch cards. No, that's yours. Think of it as a retirement bonus... but don't hold your breath. The odds of winning anything big are—well, you're more likely to get struck by lightning!"

And then he laughed with a breath full of stinky garlic, and Brett turned and left. He was holding his hand over his nose, mumbling, "P.U.!"

•••••••••••••

Brett quietly knocked on Sarah's bedroom door and heard a muffled, "Come in."

Sarah was sitting up in bed and holding an open Bible on her lap. She smiled lovingly at Brett. "Hey, Bub, how was your last day? How did it go?"

Brett shrugged, then leaned forward and gave her a gentle kiss on the forehead.

"Okay, I guess. Kind of same old, same old." Then he produced the chocolate kiss and handed it to her.

She furrowed her brow. "Hey, you can get fired for stealing these!" She paused and chuckled softly. "Well, I guess they can't fire you since you don't work there anymore. And it *is* Valentine's Day."

She popped the treat in her mouth and moaned with delight, then immediately began a hacking cough.

She coughed and coughed, nearly throwing up.

Brett reached for the glass of tap water on her bedside table and handed it to her when she'd finally finished coughing. He smiled at her tenderly, then offered her the Kleenex box.

Sarah blew her nose and wiped her eyes. "Sorry about that. You know how dairy products like chocolate coat my throat."

And she coughed again, then took another drink of water. Brett patted her leg, and the scratch ticket magically appeared in his hand. He handed it to his love as he took the water glass from her.

"Here, happy Valentine's Day. I'm betting this won't coat your throat."

Sarah's brow furrowed once again. "Bub, we can't afford this! You know that. What induced you to buy this? I mean, I appreciate the thought, but buying a lottery ticket? That's just not you."

Brett told her the story of the short, wide woman leaving it on the counter and Sahem not wanting to even touch it. And he added, "Sahem said the woman was passing through to Montana or one of the flyover states. She paid with cash, and we have no way of returning it. So scratch away, maybe it's your lucky Valentine's Day!"

And she did.

And it was.

•••••••••••

The next morning, the happy couple was having breakfast together in the kitchen. The scratch ticket had been placed in the middle of the table, propped up by the saltshaker so they could both look at it.

And they did... constantly.

The scratching had revealed quite a nice prize... well, more than a nice prize. Actually, it was a three-million-dollar prize! And the happy couple could not believe it.

It was a godsend.

Sarah's smile tugged at and twitched the corners of her mouth, and an occasional giggle was thrown in for good measure. Brett merely kept shaking his head back and forth in astonishment.

They had called the state lottery office earlier to confirm that this was, in fact, real. At the office's request, they took a snapshot of the ticket with Sarah's smartphone and sent it to them. The officials confirmed that, from what they could tell, it *was* real; the numbers matched the numbers they had on record. But they needed to see it in person to confirm officially.

But if the numbers matched what they saw in the picture, they assured Bub and Sarah, it was real.

•••••••••••••

A month later, with the first payout of the scratch ticket (nearly $750,000) securely in the bank, Sarah returned from the hospital after being diagnosed with COPD, chronic obstructive pulmonary disease.

Then, the Beckers decided to live life in the present and made plans to move to their favorite spot in the world, the Caribbean.

That would certainly help with Sarah's cough...

And her tan!

•••••••••••

Ann Marie Swanson, maiden name Noble, finished the last chocolate kiss and turned out the light, hoping to get a good night's sleep... for once. Her exhausted husband was already asleep with a happy smile on his face after once again trying to conceive their first child.

So far, to no avail.

The young couple had used up all of their savings trying expensive in vitro fertilization, but so far, no luck. Even their credit cards were maxed out, and the phone rang constantly with annoying calls from debt collectors.

Unfriendly debt collectors.

The first thing the next morning, Ann Marie made a cup of steaming coffee, and just the pleasant aroma nearly woke her up, no caffeine involved. Then she sneaked out the door into the orange sunshine while in her pajamas to pick up yesterday's mail.

She sucked in her breath and groaned despairingly as she sorted through the mail. It was bill after bill, as well as a nasty letter from the IRS threatening all sorts of terrible repercussions. On the way through the garage and back into the kitchen, she opened the big garbage can and tossed the whole bundle into the bottom of the can, just to be rid of it.

One of the unopened letters hit the side of the can and bounced off, falling at her feet. She sighed resignedly and slowly bent down to retrieve it. She was about to toss it in the trash can along with all of the other unwelcome bills... when she realized this was not a bill.

It was actually a letter, addressed to her in a scrawl that she had never seen before.

For some reason, she shivered as she put the lid on the can, then clutched the letter to her chest. Making her way back into the kitchen, she poured another cup of steaming coffee, sans creamer.

They couldn't even afford to buy her favorite creamer.

As she was sipping her second cup, she slit open the letter, which had no return address. She squinted at the tiny, scrawled handwriting.

Dear Ann Marie,

I know we have never met, and that is one of the things about my life that I will always regret, now that I am dead. Yes, when you get this letter, it means that I am probably dancing with the devil, since I lived a life that was, let's just say, not a Christian life. Even though you have never heard of nor from me, I am your long-lost uncle.

I know, I know... but really, I am. I know that your mother never mentioned me to you, and I surely don't blame her, God rest her soul. Let's just say that I was the black sheep of the family. So now, with me deceased and your father also having recently passed, you are the last of the Noble line.

So you, my dear, are the only one left to carry on Nobly.

Which is the reason I am writing this letter. The two things I did well in my life were to take out a life insurance policy and make quite a bit of money.

Which I spent on wine, women, and cocaine.

Yes, cocaine. I am the black sheep, after all.

But I never touched the life insurance policy, and it's all yours now. You are the sole beneficiary.

The name and address of my attorney and the trustee of the trust I set up for you is enclosed. He has been instructed to do whatever he can to facilitate the transfer of the money to you. By the way, he has been well paid, so there is no need for you to pay him; also, there are no taxes due on the payment. So, Ann Marie Noble, I hope this letter finds you well, and I only ask that you use part of the funds to carry on the Noble line.

Best regards,

Damon C. Noble

From the grave.

P.S. The insurance policy was initially for one million dollars, but it was invested wisely, and I'm sure it has doubled since I last looked at it.

P.P.S. Take care of yourself.

Ann Marie screamed for joy!

•••••••••••••

Banker William "Dick" Stockton looked out his office window at the golden sunlight bouncing off the tall building, as if the sun were playing ping-pong with the structures. It was Friday afternoon, and it had been an unusual week, with good news and bad news all packed into seven days.

At the office, and at home.

The good news at home was that his daughter Chelsea had been accepted into Stanford University in Palo Alto, California. The bad news was that she had no scholarships and the tuition was astronomical.

Dick already had twins in college at the University of Wisconsin, Madison and his oldest daughter was just finishing up her engineering program at MIT. Looking at his bank statement, Dick had no idea how he was going to pay for Chelsea's education. Not only was he maxed out on parent plus student loans, but he also was not getting his credit cards paid off on a timely basis, which for him was a cardinal sin.

For God's sake, he was a banker.

He looked at the statement and sighed and shivered. He was making $80,000 a year with a $15,000 bonus, and it was not nearly enough. He was a vice president, which sounded good... but at a bank, *everyone* was a vice president.

He chuckled to himself. Hell, pretty soon the tellers would be made vice presidents!

It also had been a stressful week at the bank. His friend and mentor, the bank president, had died on Tuesday after a short battle with lung cancer. Barrett Archer Beckett Jr. had died far too young at only 58 years of age.

Probably sneaking a cigarette before he passed.

Barrett had been a great friend and a good mentor. He'd been film-star handsome, but of only average intelligence. His father, the bank's chairman of the board, was the one blessed with above-average smarts. It was Barrett Sr. who had started the bank with a loan from his father nearly 40 years ago.

And the bank had flourished.

Dick's boss, Payne Stewart, had been telling everyone who would listen—including board members—that he was next in line for the presidency. After all, he had just closed the largest deal that the bank had ever seen.

Dick opened his canted drawer and slid his bank statement into the shallow drawer inside of it. He sighed again, his hostility nearly bubbling out of his ears. He wanted to stand up on his desk and release a primal scream. He knew Payne Stewart had nothing to do with the big sale. He, William Stockton, had put it together. He had courted the prospect for nearly three years, buying the committee members lunch and/or dinner on a regular basis. He sent wine baskets on their birthdays and had even made a generous wedding donation to the president's daughter's wedding.

Out of his own pocket.

And now, Payne was taking all of the credit for the sale just because he sat in on the final presentation. He hadn't said a word during Dick's presentation, but he'd smiled and winked at everyone on the committee. Additionally, Payne was telling everyone who would listen that he was going to terminate Dick now that Barrett was no longer around to protect him. He had never liked the fact that Barrett had taken Dick under his wing.

So he hated Dick, passionately.

Dick heard voices just outside of his office door. It was his assistant, and she was talking to someone whose voice sounded familiar.

"Yes, sir, it's nice to see you, sir! And yes, he *is* in today. Please take all you want; those are left over from Valentine's Day."

Barrett Archer Beckett Sr. stuck his head around the doorframe and smiled as he unwrapped a chocolate kiss and popped it into his mouth. He was even more attractive than his son, partly because his platinum-gray hair gave off an afterglow that seemed almost metallic.

"Hello, William," the chairman said. He entered the office and pointed to a visitor's chair. "Do you mind if I sit?"

Dick, who was standing pretty much at attention, motioned towards the chair. "Please do, sir."

He extended his hand for a handshake. Instead of giving a shake, however, the chairman put a chocolate kiss in his hand with a half-smile.

"Here, try this. I've been eating everything in sight since Barrett passed; you can save me from myself."

Dick sat back down and slowly unwrapped the kiss.

Barrett Sr. looked around the spacious office and chuckled. "Nice office." He paused. "We don't pay guys like you nearly well enough, but we give people nice offices and nice titles."

He grimaced. "Like you could actually spend a title."

Dick shrugged, not knowing what to say.

"I thought I would stop by and see how you were doing, William?" the chairman asked after a moment. He was smiling, but soon his smile faltered. "I know you were good friends with Barrett."

Dick pursed his lips, nodded, and sighed once again. He looked out the window to see that the sun was winning the ping-pong game with the tall buildings.

"Yes, sir, he was the best. A first-class friend and an even better mentor. He taught me everything I know about banking."

As Dick inhaled and held it, the chairman shrugged. "Well, I'm not so sure about that… Barrett was not the brightest bulb on the Christmas tree, and he knew it, but he *was* good at picking smart people to support him."

And he hesitated. "I will tell you this: he thought the world of you, and he made it known to me before he died."

He hesitated again.

"You know, he was on the board of directors, and even while he was dying, he actually phone conferenced into the last board meeting. And he let everyone know how much he thought of you—and more."

Dick sat up straight and popped the kiss into his mouth without even realizing it.

"Anyway, William, I'm here to let you know that, in spite of what Payne Stewart is telling everyone, he is not going to get the president's job."

The chairman slowly unwrapped another chocolate kiss, held it to his nose, and popped it into his mouth.

"Don't you love the aroma of chocolate?"

The chairman chewed contently and looked out the window as he continued. "In fact, the Payne-in-the-ass is cleaning out his desk as we sit here eating chocolate and will soon be escorted out of the building by security."

And the chairman damn near giggled.

"Thanks to Barrett, we know you closed the largest deal this bank has ever secured. He told the board how you courted the Beamen Company for over three years and used your own funds to influence the committee members."

The chairman beamed at Dick as if he were his son.

"And I'm here on behalf of the board to give you our heartfelt thanks."

He looked around the office. "As of today, your salary will be $250,000, and if we are profitable—and we certainly will be, thanks to you—your annual bonus will be at least $100,000 a year. Also, for closing the deal, you will be getting a commission of $50,000. It will be in your next paycheck."

The chairman stood and placed another kiss in his mouth, then turned and went to the door.

He stopped. The handsome man, smelling like chocolate, turned around and glanced around Dick's office.

"Oh, by the way, you need to move offices. You are going to move into Barrett's old office."

And the chairman winked at William and finished simply, *"Mr. President."*

Homeless... But Then...

The 50-caliber machine gun fired with a rigorous staccato cracking sound that was felt more than heard. The soldier felt it in his diaphragm and down into his bowels.

BAM

RAT-A-TAT

TAT

And then all hell broke loose.

•••••••••••••

One of the last things he remembered was sitting above his buddies on top of the MAT-V and manning the powerful machine gun. Now he was sitting on the side of the road, baking in the relentless Afghanistan sun with annoying drips of sweat sliding off of his nose. He was cradling the head of one of his direct reports in his lap.

The man was dead, but he held him as if he were still alive. The MAT-V, blown to smithereens, now lay in the ditch in front of him—which was just as well, since it provided a bit of cover. The rest of the convoy sped past him without a glance as they zeroed in on the target: an ancient farmhouse on a patch of land that had once grown pomegranates and grapes. It had been abandoned and left to the Afghan rebels long ago.

But he was out of the fight. He had been hit in the forehead just below his helmet, and he knew he had a concussion. Additionally, a bullet had ripped through his calf, and he was bleeding profusely into his boot. He could barely walk.

Or could he?

He looked down at his dead buddy's M4 Carbine and smiled as he picked it up.

Maybe he could.

●●●●●●●●●●●●●

Memories of the Afghan sun were all that the soldier had left as he pulled the ancient sleeping bag up and over his face, nearly cutting off all oxygen flow.

It was bitterly cold in Minneapolis, and the cardboard box that he now considered home did little to keep the 15-below January cold at bay.

He shivered and pulled his winter coat tighter around himself. The coat, compliments of Goodwill, was now too large for him, as he had lost nearly thirty pounds since being sent home from the fight.

The soldier had spent time in the VA on the outskirts of Minneapolis, Minnesota. But his memory of that was more than a bit cloudy; in fact, he had been told he had amnesia. The doctors said that it had to do with post-traumatic stress disorder, and he had no reason to doubt them. They had done a nice follow-up job with the calf wound he had suffered in Afghanistan… a wound that he didn't remember receiving at all, which was just as well.

But hell, it still hurt a year later.

The cold didn't help, either. As he pushed the corner of the discarded sleeping bag open a bit to let in some much-needed oxygen, he shivered at the chill that crept into the bag. It was nearing dawn, and he had not slept well at all, which was now normal for him. And by God, he was hungry—he had not eaten since yesterday afternoon when he stopped at McDonald's. He moaned at the memory of the Big Mac and the quarter pounder with fries he'd eaten as he pulled the old coat tighter around himself. He had been getting a free meal from the restaurant for months now, ever since he had saved the manager from an irate customer.

At the beginning of that particular incident, he had been dumpster diving and was munching on some nasty frozen fries when he passed by the side window and witnessed an angry customer throwing his meal over the counter at the manager. The man was about to fling a strawberry shake at the manager's head when the soldier busted through the door and tackled him from behind, smashing the large man's head into the counter and then down onto the dirty floor. The soldier was sixty pounds lighter than the belligerent customer, but with his training and his PTSD anger that was always ready to bubble up, the angry customer was no match for him.

In fact, the soldier had damn near killed the guy.

But the manager and a few employees had quickly taken control of the situation, sending the soldier on his way with a hefty sack of burgers before the police arrived. And since then, the soldier had been getting a free bag filled with a hot, tasty meal once a day.

Albeit, it was always to go.

The former soldier's name was Pier Truchon, and he was cold, underfed, and angry at the world. He felt hopeless and had constant negative feelings about the future. He knew that his name was Pier Truchon because that was the name in the wallet in his back pocket. The wallet had served him well when he had returned home, until the credit cards had been canceled abruptly and his three hundred dollars had all been spent.

Pier smiled in spite of the cold. An image flashed in his memory of a beautiful dark-haired woman with eyes like sparkling emeralds. The picture was being kept warm by his left buttock. What was written on the back of it was what kept Pier going:

I love you. Please come back to me.

So Pier was doing just that, even though he had no idea where she was and how to find her. If someone with those emerald eyes could love him, then maybe, just maybe...

...life was worth living.

•••••••••••••

Pier woke up with a start.

He had been dreaming a nice warm dream. He was back in Afghanistan, and he had picked up his buddy's rifle, hooked a tailgate ride on a passing Hummer, and single-handedly stormed the pomegranate farm. Not only did he vividly remember blasting open the front door and hosing down some of the Afghan rebels, but he also remembered the *thud* of the Arges Type HG 84 hand grenade that he lobbed into the upper level.

It was the thud in the dream that caused him to wake. As he lay there, the front of his makeshift home was opened and a police officer with a mustache coated in frozen snot poked his flashlight into the cardboard box.

The movement startled Pier, making him angry. The old Pier had never been startled. He had been on guard for danger, but never startled.

The cop's icy lips moved as he mumbled something like, "Hey, buddy, are you still alive in here?"

Pier dampened his all-too-common rising anger, and his military training took over seamlessly.

"Yes, sir, alive and well."

The police officer scoped out the tiny cardboard home and shook his head. "Are you sure you don't want to come with me, soldier? The Salvation Army has rooms and will give you a hot meal, and they have an opening."

Pier clutched his coat around him, not appreciating the cold that the officer was letting into his shelter.

"No, sir. Been there, done that. I guess I don't do well with people."

The officer looked at Pier's gaunt, drawn face. "When's the last time you ate, soldier?"

Pier felt his anger rise once again but tamped it down, knowing that the cop was simply doing his duty.

"I'm good, officer; ate quite a bit yesterday."

The officer shrugged as he backed out of the shelter.

"Okay, if you say so… but I'm going to look in on you. Most homeless folks have more sense and come in out of the cold."

He closed the door and hurried off to his squad car, shouting to no one in particular, "Damn, it's freaking cold out here!"

●●●●●●●●●●●●

Two days later, the weather broke. The morning high reached nearly 38 degrees, and Pier actually slept in... if you could call sleeping until 6:30 sleeping in.

It was Tuesday, and he knew that the McDonald's manager had the early shift on Tuesday. So he roused himself and headed out for a breakfast of one of his favorite meals, the Mac's breakfast burritos.

With lots of hot sauce.

He slipped into the side door of the fast-food restaurant, and the manager motioned to him from the back. Pier stood in line, and the manager signaled him over and handed him a steaming cup of coffee.

"Good morning, soldier. What would you like today?"

Pier smiled one of his rare smiles. "Well, sir, if it's okay with you, how about one of your burritos?"

The manager, Todd, smiled. He knew it was one of the sol-dier's favorites. "Absolutely, how about three... and extra hot sauce?"

Pier stood up ramrod straight and saluted. "Yes, sir, that would be most appreciated."

As Pier sipped his scalding coffee, he watched the rest of the customers. Most were headed into work, but a few were moms with kids getting a head start on the day. Todd returned with a full bag and handed it to Pier.

"I put a couple of leftover apple pies from yesterday in there," he said with a good-natured grin. "We need to fatten you up, soldier."

After that, Pier headed back to his home to enjoy his nutritious meal.

He had pulled one of the apple treats out of the bag and was munching on it as he approached the bridge that his makeshift home was under. That was when he stopped, suddenly confronted by four young men.

"Hey, bro," a short, squat, acne-scarred young man greeted him. "How nice of you—looks like you got me breakfast," he added, lunging toward Pier and snatching the bag out of his hand.

Pier exploded.

He was thirty pounds lighter and hadn't worked out in months, but his military training immediately kicked in. It was like riding a bike.

As the leader of the group leaned in toward him, Pier did the same and headbutted the man viciously.

The man's nose exploded in crimson, and Pier's breakfast—the cherished burritos—went flying. Pier then turned his attention to the second man, a tall guy with a mustache that no adolescent Mexican would have been proud of. As he slid toward the former soldier, Pier turned sideways and kicked out his right leg in a leg chop just under the man's knee. Ligaments snapped, and the man squealed like a three-year-old señorita.

And the fight was over.

The two other men did the right thing and scampered off the bridge, living to fight another day. Pier looked down at his now squashed and cold breakfast. The bleeding gang member was on his knees in the cold, still trying to stop the bloody flow. Pier pushed him to the ground face first and yanked his oversized wallet out of his low-rider pants. He opened it, finding to his delight that it contained nearly one hundred dollars. He quickly put the bills in his pocket and tossed the wallet back at the man. He stooped and grabbed a burrito, then turned the guy over, tossing the squashed burrito on top of his crimson jacket.

"Here, you paid for this. Enjoy."

• • • • • • • • • • • •

Pier ate well for three days. In addition to his fast food from McDonald's, he hiked a couple of miles and ate at his favorite restaurant, Perkins. Low cost, lots of food, and a free piece of pie.

Excellent.

In the meantime, the sub-zero temperature rose to forty degrees for a day, melting snow and slush. For the next two days, the temperature dropped to the upper twenties—which was still plenty warm, compared to twenty below.

Pier was returning from another trip to McDonald's, anticipating the Big Macs and double quarter pounder with cheese in his bag as he trundled over the bridge that he lived under. He spotted an undamaged burrito hot sauce packet nestled against the side of the bridge. Thinking that it might be a nice change of pace instead of ketchup, he headed over and picked it up.

He was just opening his food bag when he looked over the side of the bridge.

He saw a police squad car below him, which wasn't a surprise, because the mustachioed officer had said that he would check on him. But what *did* surprise him was that he saw the gangbanger with the broken nose pointing a Smith & Wesson handgun at the officer, who was still seated behind the steering wheel.

The gang member was speaking loudly, as if he wanted his buddies to hear what he was saying. "Well, well, I get a twofer—that goddamn homeless soldier, but first I get to kill a *pig*," he said, slowly squeezing the trigger.

Pier felt the anger rise inside of him and visibly trembled— and not because of the cold.

The soldier wasted no time, tossing his bag of goodies at the gang member and leaping over the rail to follow it. The bag of food exploded on the man's head just as he shot at the officer. Burgers and fries went everywhere—and the bullet, off the mark because of the bag of food, simply blew out the front window, leaving the "pig" unscathed.

The gangbanger looked up just as Pier landed on him head first, snapping his neck and sending him to the frozen ground.

He was dead before he hit the ice.

Pier landed on the man's chest with a whomp as the Smith & Wesson dropped from the man's hand. Pier strained to grab it, but the handgun was out of his reach, so he leapt up and retrieved it. Turning toward the remaining gang members, he was surprised to see one of the guys pointing another handgun at him.

Unfortunately, Pier had picked up the Smith & Wesson by the short barrel. As he reversed the familiar handgun into the proper position, he slipped on the ice… just as the man fired at him.

Pier's gun went flying, and his head smacked into the cold bumper of the squad car. He was out like a light.

In the meantime, the police officer had jumped into the fray and put a bullet smack-dab into the middle of the armed gang member's chest.

The others turned and ran.

The officer, Elijah Washington, thought about running them down with his car, but quickly gave up the idea and radioed in his position, requesting an ambulance. He hurried back out of his squad car and knelt down by the unconscious soldier.

He cradled Pier's head in his lap as he waited for help to arrive.

"Hey soldier, you saved my life!"

•••••••••••

Pier Truchon woke up in bed, feeling nice and warm... but with a splitting headache. He was back in the VA hospital, and a nurse was standing next to him with a smile on her face.

"Well, hero, welcome back to the VA. We missed you, soldier. Where the heck did you disappear to?"

Pier shrugged as best he could and simply said, "Could I have something for a headache? My head is killing me."

The nurse nodded. "I can get you Tylenol, but not Advil."

Pier shrugged again and looked beyond her as Officer Elijah Washington stepped into the doorway.

"Hey, soldier, nice to have you back with the living. I've been waiting for you to wake up. I just wanted to say thanks for saving my life. That was incredible. So thank you!" the other man gushed.

Pier shrugged a third time. It was getting to be a habit.

"Not a problem, officer; I had a run-in with those gang-bangers a few days before, and if you weren't there, they would have killed me. So I'm thinking we're even."

Elijah smiled. "Well, two of 'em aren't going to be bothering anyone anymore."

The nurse returned with the Tylenol. "Officer, we need to send you on your way. This man needs to sleep."

Officer Washington winked at Pier. "I'll see you soon, soldier, and hey, they have nice rooms here for vets here and three squares a day. Let's not go back to living under that damn bridge."

Pier shrugged, of course, and said nothing.

•••••••••••

The former soldier woke up again the next morning. His headache was nearly gone, and he was famished. "Boy, a breakfast burrito or three would be tasty," he muttered.

A new nurse appeared out of nowhere. "Hey, I hear you're quite the hero. Congratulations!"

Pier began to shrug again, but he stopped himself. "Well, how about if this hero gets some breakfast? I'm starving."

The nurse nodded. "I figured you might be, so I ordered for you, and I doubled up on everything. It will be here soon. But in the meantime, someone is waiting for you to wake up."

Pier grimaced. "Who is that? I don't really know anybody in Minneapolis."

The nurse burst into laughter. "I'm not so sure about that. Wait till you see your guest."

As she scooted out the door, Pier heard her say, "Good morning, Governor. He is awake and ready to see you."

Pier sat up ramrod straight in his bed.

The governor entered the room, and Pier sucked in his breath. He blinked his eyes and exhaled. The man standing in front of him was... well... him!

The man smiled a loving smile and stood with his hat in his hand at the end of Pier's hospital bed. "Welcome back, Richard. You sure gave us a scare for a while. We had no idea where you went."

The soldier shook his head. "I'm not Richard; I'm Pier Truchon."

The governor laughed. "No, trust me on this one—you are my brother, Richard Dayton."

He smiled again. "Pier Truchon was killed in action in Afghanistan more than six months ago. You had his wallet in your hip pocket, but no, Richard, you are definitely not Pier Truchon."

After a pause, he exclaimed, "You are my twin!"

•••••••••••••

The days flew by; Richard Dayton was moved to a room for returning soldiers and was feeling much, much better. He had restarted his anxiety medication, and he was actually feeling human and sociable. He kidded with the other soldiers at mess and even told a few jokes. It was like old times, and he started to think about the future. With his wound, it was not necessary for him to return to the fight, but he had no idea what he was going to do. His days of living under a bridge were over, and he shuddered at the memory of it. Officer Washington had stopped in on occasion and even chauffeured Richard to his old McDonald's, where he did indeed have three breakfast burritos with extra hot sauce. Todd the manager was delighted to see him, and when Officer Washington told the story of how Richard had saved him from the gangbangers, he cheered out loud.

"Breakfast is on me, Mr. Dayton—and please don't be a stranger!"

After breakfast, Officer Elijah Washington did not drive back to the Veterans Administration. Rather, he drove up to the governor's mansion and pulled into the circular driveway.

Richard tilted his head and pursed his lips at his new buddy Elijah. "What are we doing here?"

The officer smiled. "It's your new home, at least for a few weeks or so. Your brother insisted, and he is waiting for you upstairs. Also, you're being thrown out of the VA. Lots of soldiers are returning from Afghanistan, and they need your room." Elijah laughed. "Unless you want to go back to living under the bridge?"

Richard opened the door of the squad car. "No, I guess I'll stay here—been there, done that."

•••••••••••••

The stay at the governor's mansion went well. The former soldier ate well, worked out in the weight room in the basement of the mansion, and regained the weight he had lost. He had gone shopping at the Mall of America, which was a mistake, since everyone thought he was his brother, Mark Dayton. He even signed a few autographs with a mischievous grin on his face. But he did in fact get nicely outfitted, and the Army had seen fit to reissue his uniform with space for the Congressional Medal of Honor, which would be presented to him by the president at the White House. Prior to that, the governor was sponsoring a dinner dance at the mansion where the Minneapolis police were going to present Richard with the Officer Medal of Valor and Honor instead of the Citizen Medal of Valor. This was the first time it had ever been done, and the rank and file wholeheartedly supported it.

After all, Richard had saved one of their own.

Richard had looked at the guest list and been delighted that dozens of his former friends had been invited. He felt especially gratified that his commanding officer, Major Mike Murray, was flying in from Afghanistan to attend. The band was one of Richard's favorites, a local group called Rusty Sunset that played lots of old rock tunes, including lots of songs by the Eagles.

His favorite band.

The evening of the party had arrived, and Richard was dilly-dallying in his spacious room. He was ready to go—shoes polished, pants creased, medals shined—but he hesitated. He closed his eyes, thinking about the past few months and all that he had been through. He certainly didn't ever want to live under a bridge again, nor forget who he was... but at the academy, he'd been told that anything that doesn't kill you only makes you stronger.

And he certainly *was* stronger. He pulled Pier's wallet out of his pocket and opened it. The picture of the beautiful woman was the only thing left in it. It was in the slot where a driver's license would have gone. The soldiers in the field were cautioned to never take their licenses with them into a fight.

Richard held the photograph up to the light and felt a tingle run down his spine.

It all came rushing back to him. The woman was Pier's fiancée, Dominique Beaumont. Pier had talked about her as if she were a princess; in fact, that's what he had called her, "princess." Her olive skin was smooth and unblemished. Her nose was perky, and her eyes sparkled with intelligence and compassion.

Compassion.

That was the very word that Pier had used. She was incredibly compassionate; in fact, he had compared her to Richard. "You are two of the most compassionate people I have ever met. And you will never meet her until I'm married to her, because she would dump me in a heartbeat once she met you. She thinks she has enough compassion for both of us, but I'm not so sure. I don't treat people well, and she knows that."

Richard shook his head at the old memory.

"But Richard, I've told her all about you, and if I somehow don't make it back, she is to look you up. I told her that you would take care of her."

Richard inhaled deeply, remembering the moment. Pier had then said, "So please do that."

•••••••••••

Richard finally went down to the ballroom. The band was doing a sound check and people were already lined up at the free bar. His brother Mark met him in the wide doorway where he was greeting the attendees. Mark made no comment about Richard shirking his duties by skipping the meet-and-greet. He was simply happy to have his old brother back and functioning well.

Mark was chatting with Major Mike Murray, who extended his hand for a shake. Richard instead saluted, and the major returned it with a crisp salute of his own.

Then the major did something unusual—he gave Richard a hug.

And the soldier damn near cried.

"I've heard about what you did, rushing the farmhouse in Afghanistan in spite of being so wounded you could hardly walk. And now?" The major looked around and nodded to the police officers setting up on stage to present Richard with their own medal. "You come back and are a hero again. Soldier, I am proud of you." And he stepped back and saluted once again.

An embarrassed Richard Dayton simply shrugged.

After that, Richard made his way through the crowd greeting people, both friends and strangers alike. He marveled at what the PTSD medication was doing for him, but the doctors at the VA had said that they had seen wonderful results with the drug… as long as people remembered to take it religiously. So far, so good.

Richard was again making his way through the growing crowd when the police commissioner's chief of staff tapped on the end of his microphone.

"Hello, hello, can I have your attention please? Has anyone seen our guest of honor?"

The crowd around Richard pointed at him, and Richard raised his hand. "Well, Mr. Dayton, please come on up here."

And the crowd parted around him like the Red Sea.

Climbing nimbly up the side stairs, Richard shook hands with the police commissioner, who apparently liked Scotch, as his breath reeked of it. Next was his friend Elijah Washington, who simply gave Richard a hug and whispered in his ear, "Thanks again, my friend."

The commissioner strode to the podium, quieted the crowd, and then very elegantly and precisely described the encounter with the gangbangers and how Richard had saved Officer Washington from certain death. His chief of staff handed a shiny medal to the commissioner, who pinned it on Richard's chest along with his other medals. Richard wondered if that would be okay with the army, and he glanced down at Major Murray, who was beaming and giving him the thumbs up.

The commissioner turned back to the microphone. "I now present you with our guest of honor, Mr. Richard Dayton."

The crowd went wild.

Then they did something unexpected, perhaps set off by his brother. They started to chant, "Governor Richard, Governor Richard, Governor Richard!"

Richard smiled... and nodded approvingly.

Epilogue

Appropriately, Richard Dayton announced his candidacy for governor on Veterans' Day, with his new bride Dominique Beaumont at his side. Given the vast wealth of his family, he sought no donations, asking his supporters to "do something nice for someone else." That was Dominique's idea.

Richard won the election in a landslide, and rumor had it that, when his term was finished, he was going to announce his candidacy for:

President of the United States.

Barely Alive and Grateful

Bartholomew "Bee" Roberts, an aspiring beekeeper, had just moved his young family to Wyoming because of the state's preponderance of bees. Bart, as he was known, and his wife Ruth had settled just outside of Cheyenne. They moved into a small log cabin and had two dozen beehives on the property. The happy couple had a precocious, red-headed, freckled three-year-old named Mary Lou and a six-month-old son. In spite of Ruth's objections, Bart had christened him Beetholomew. The little tot's nickname, of course, was Bee.

It was Thanksgiving and Ruth was busy preparing the meal—roast chicken, potatoes, carrots, peas, and gravy, followed by Bart's favorite: honey pumpkin pie. He affectionately patted his wife's behind as she stood at the stove, stirring the gravy. He gave her a kiss on the cheek and hurried out the door, carrying his bee-netting headgear. He whistled a song as he strode confidently through the small forest between his cabin and the hives. Several restaurants in Cheyenne were using his honey to make honey biscuits, honey cheesecake, and baklava, a Middle Eastern dessert. Bart was planning to add another dozen hives next spring and eventually have more than one hundred, once the children were able to help. After all, people never tire of honey.

Bart sniffed the air. Smoke was coming his way and it appeared to be coming from the field where he kept his hives. As he emerged from the forest, he pulled the net down over his face and stopped in his tracks, anger rising in his gut.

At the far end of the row of hives, three Indian squaws and two bucks were harvesting Bart's precious honey and, from the looks of it, they'd been at it a long time. The smallest woman was filling up a huge crock while the other two held smaller bowls in their hands. As Bart started towards them the trespassers looked up, startled. One of the women turned towards Bart, while one of her male companions released an arrow that came close to piercing Bart's hat.

Wasting no time, Bart headed towards the mountain to lead the Indians away from his family. As he ran, he discarded his hat. When he reached the foot of the mountain, he glanced behind him. The woman was right behind him, holding a small crock of honey in her right hand and screeching as she ran. Bart turned, stumbled, and fell flat on his face. She was on him in a heartbeat and as soon as he tried to stand up, she smashed the crock into the side of his skull and he slumped to the ground.

The woman hurled herself at him, her claws ready to rip his face open. Bart reached up and backhanded her and she went down in a heap. He stood up shakily and an arrow thudded into the small tree next to him. Heart pounding, he ran even faster towards the mountain, slipping and sliding as he passed a small cave. He stopped to catch his breath and looked over his shoulder. Even though the Indians were still out of sight, Bart could hear their whooping coming closer so he ducked quickly into the cave.

Bart could hear the Indians just outside the cave entrance so he pushed even farther into the narrow space. He came to an abrupt stop when he came upon the largest bear he'd ever seen. The bear was sound asleep and Bart turned, thinking perhaps he should deal with the Indians instead of being a meal for the bear. But at that moment, an arrow passed by his arm, followed by another. Bart tiptoed around the bear and headed for the rear of the cave. One of the Indian men followed behind him, whooping and hollering, waking the sleeping bear.

The bear raised its massive head, got to its feet, and charged the Indian. The warrior turned around, dropped his bow, and tried to escape, but the bear grabbed him by the buttocks and began to shake him. As the man screamed, Bart moved deeper into the cave. He watched as the bear released its grip on the warrior and slashed at him, ripping the back of his legs as he crawled towards the sunshine. The bear followed the warrior to the entrance of the cave and watched as the man threw himself down the mountain and rolled to safety.

The massive animal stood up on its hind legs and let out a thunderous roar. Then it turned around and re-entered the cave to find a trembling Bart, hands folded in prayer and making peace with the good Lord. The beast stopped and sniffed the air. It moved slowly towards Bart with a low growl. Bart closed his eyes, knelt down, and made the sign of the cross. The bear went quiet, sniffed Bart's ear, and began to lick the honey off his ears and neck, growling in ecstasy.

The bear finished licking the sweet treat as Bart opened his eyes, preparing to die. The beast stood up on its hind legs, gave Bart a bear hug, and licked his ear once more. Then it turned around, plopped to the ground, and promptly fell asleep with what appeared to be a smile on its face.

Bart tiptoed past the bear and walked out into the sunshine with an even bigger smile on his face, giving thanks for being alive... bearly.

Corona Without a Lime

Susan Swenson was enjoying being retired. After many years as an emergency room nurse, followed by ten more in the cardiovascular rehabilitation unit, she was happy to have turned in her scrubs. She and her husband Eric had just purchased their dream house and she was busy turning it into a home. They'd finally taken a long-overdue trip to Italy and Germany and now they were preparing to visit old friends in Limpopo, Africa. It was home to the Anopheles, a malaria-bearing mosquito, so Susan had stocked up on hydroxychloroquine tablets.

Then COVID-19 hit, and life was turned on its head with the imposed social distancing restrictions of no travel, no church, and no restaurants. Susan was 66 years old, so the experts said she was at risk. And maybe she was.

Three months ago, when the word Corona only referred to a beer, she'd had a fever and a nagging cough with some wheezing. She'd also lost her sense of taste and smell. The symptoms disappeared after four weeks, but now Susan realized that she might have been one of the first victims of the virus.

She felt fine now, so when the clarion call went out to retired nurses and doctors to return to duty, she answered, albeit reluctantly, and over Eric's objections. "What if you catch it again and bring it home?" he said worriedly. Susan shared his fears but when her former colleagues put on their scrubs again, she was shamed into thrusting herself into the pandemic. Hell, Eric has good life insurance, she thought to herself. She returned to the hospital, but since the rehab unit was closed, she became an intensive care nurse.

For the first few days, Susan tagged along with an experienced ICU nurse to get a feel for the demands of the unit. But as the case numbers climbed and nurse after nurse contracted the virus, she was quickly thrust into the front line. She worked nearly eighteen hours a day, seven days a week from morning to night, eating little but trying to keep hydrated. At the end of two weeks, she stood on her scale and laughed. She'd lost almost fifteen pounds—the hard way.

One Saturday morning a familiar face appeared in the ICU. Grace Dawson, age 89, had been a patient of Susan's many years ago. She'd come to the cardio rehab clinic after a heart event and was a delight. She never missed a visit, followed orders to the letter, expressed her opinions in class, and stood up to the men who were arguing over what news channel to watch. Susan grinned as she remembered Grace quietly picking up the remote and changing the channel to HGTV. But, because it was Grace, no one complained.

Grace's husband had died of cancer at the still-young age of 71. They'd had four children but two had died, one at childbirth and the other, her only son, at the age of 30 in a car crash. He'd been a financial planner, so he'd left behind a large life insurance policy that named Grace as the primary beneficiary. The coverage amounted to the tune of one million dollars.

After a long period of grieving, Grace had been reborn. She traveled the world, taking along one of her daughters whenever she could. One was a history professor and the other was an occasional waitress with a cocaine habit. Although they were no longer speaking to each other, Grace loved them both.

It was on her last trip, a cruise, that Grace caught the coronavirus. The ship had been turned away from country after country before she and the other sick passengers were finally helicoptered to an airport and flown back to the U.S.

Now Grace was in the ICU, a shadow of her former self and holding on by a thread. She had a very high fever and her lungs were filled with fluid. She was short of breath and had a hacking cough. But she recognized Susan immediately and gave her a wink and a squeeze with her hand. "I guess I shouldn't have taken that cruise but the deals were incredible!" she said between coughs.

Susan was tired, overwhelmed, and beginning to develop a cough of her own, but she made sure to check on Grace, who was receiving only fluids and oxygen. Susan and her colleagues privately wondered why the governor had forbidden the administration of malaria drugs, since they'd helped some patients in New York.

Grace was going steadily downhill. Late on a Thursday night, a priest was summoned to perform last rites and Susan stood by quietly as Grace struggled to breathe. When the priest left the room, Susan quickly took two malaria pills from a bottle in her purse, dissolved them in a glass of water, and helped Grace to drink. She tucked the covers around her favorite patient and sat down in a chair next to her bed. She prayed over her and then fell into a deep sleep.

Early the next morning, Susan awoke to find Grace touching her on the shoulder, her eyes sparkling. "Good morning, Susan! You can go home. I'm feeling much better!" She smiled and held up her water glass. "Cheers, and God bless you."

The Cracked Easter

Walt Mealy was out for his morning run, and he wanted to hurry it along. After all, it was Easter Sunday, and he needed to hide his children's eggs. His girls were seven and four years old and, along with his wife Sarah, they were the loves of his life.

Walt took a different route than usual, deciding to run around Lake Calhoun. Mansions surrounded the lake—as well as some wannabe mansions.

It had been a tough year. Walt had been laid off in February, forcing Sarah to go back to work. Her job paid the bills, but just barely.

Her birthday was coming up the week after Easter, and he was caught between a rock and a hard place. Walt needed less than twenty-five dollars to pay for the diamond engagement ring that he hadn't been able to afford when he'd proposed. It was on layaway and the remaining portion needed to be paid off quickly or he would forfeit over five hundred dollars. Those were the terms that he had agreed to, the terms that allowed him to get a substantial discount on the ring—as long as he paid his portion on time.

And he regretted that decision now that he had been laid off.

But he put the negative thoughts out of his mind; after all, it was a glorious Easter Sunday. The dawn morphed into a beautiful raspberry and orange cloudless sunrise with the promise of warm weather and chocolate bunnies for his daughters.

He had been running for less than a quarter mile when he passed what was called the 3M Mansion. It had been built over sixty years ago by one of the major investors in 3M, Lucius Ordway. The stately home was also nicknamed the Post-It Note Mansion, after one of the products that the company was famous for.

As Walt ran past the home, he spotted something gleaming in the grass next to the decorative two-foot-high wrought iron fence surrounding the front of the mansion. He slowed, then stopped and backtracked, smiling as he picked up a shiny new quarter. He thought to himself, *A good luck omen! And hell, every quarter helps at this point.*

He started to continue his run, but then paused as he spotted another gleam just on the other side of the fence. Walt moved tentatively across the grass and looked down at the gleaming object, which was indeed another quarter. He looked around him, stepped over the low fence, and picked it up. As he turned to leave, he spotted another gleam in the grass and stepped closer to it. *A silver dollar!*

Now Walt was intrigued. He looked at the sidewalk just a few paces away and thought that perhaps a runner—or more likely, a bicyclist—had crashed here and spewed the shiny coins across the lawn. At least that's what he wanted to believe. Walt looked all around him and spotted one gleam after another as he quickly zigzagged back and forth across the freshly mown, sweet-smelling lawn, picking up coins of all denominations. He found nickels and dimes and a few more quarters. And then—*eureka*—he hit the jackpot as he spotted a large coin that was nearly buried in the lawn. Walt reached down and pulled it out of the soil.

He let out a whoop.

It was an old twenty-dollar gold coin, worth more than all the nickels and dimes and quarters that he had gathered and put in his running pouch. A lot more! He wiped off the coin on his shirt and added it to his running pouch. Then he spotted another gleam as he moved a bit closer to the mansion.

This time he was disappointed, finding just another measly quarter. It was lying next to a plastic pink Easter egg that had somehow cracked open and disgorged it. Shinier than the other coins, it was as brand new as a coin could be, minted this year, 2020.

Finally, it hit him. The coins were part of an Easter egg hunt. He glanced guiltily toward the Post-It Note Mansion and spotted numerous plastic Easter eggs of all colors. The dew coated them as they awaited the eager egg hunters.

Walt sighed. *How could I have been so stupid?* he wondered.

And he sighed again.

Walt quickly bent down to return the quarter to the pink egg as a Minneapolis police car quietly pulled up to the curb, its red and blue lights flashing. Two uniformed officers got out and stepped over the short fence, their faces unamused. One of the officers looked up at the second story of the mansion and waved, then gestured for the person behind the window to come down. The other officer examined Walt as she put her hand on the butt of her revolver.

"Are you armed, sir?"

Walt almost fainted.

"Uh... no, sir—I mean, ma'am. Why would I be armed?"

He quickly added, "I'm just out for a run."

The other officer snickered. "Uh-huh, sure you were. And you just happened to be starting the Easter egg hunt a little early, weren't you?"

Just then, the current owner of the 3M Mansion hurried into the yard. He was clad in flannel pajamas and slippers and holding a steaming cup of coffee that threw off the delightful aroma of mocha.

"Hello, officers, thank you for coming so quickly! I've been watching this man while I waited for you, and he has a pouch full of money that was supposed to go to the kids from the orphanage."

Walt took a deep breath. "I can explain."

He took off his running pouch and handed it to the home-owner.

The homeowner snorted, spilling coffee on his pajamas. "Explain? Explain what? You are trespassing and robbing the kids!"

He turned to the officers. "Lock him up! The children will be here in less than an hour, and I need to shave and shower."

As the officers moved toward Walt, the trespasser held up his hand. "Wait, stop. This is all a mistake," he explained, glancing down at the pink egg at his feet. "I was putting them back; I didn't realize this was for an egg hunt."

Quickly, he told the story of seeing the initial gleam and then picking up the coins one after the other with the aim of paying off the loan on the engagement ring.

It seemed like once he started, he couldn't stop his explanation. The officers both shook their heads when Walt was finished with his story, and the homeowner waved his coffee cup in Walt's face.

"Yeah, right! Putting them back, that's nonsense," he said, shifting the pouch full of coins to his other hand.

Walt pointed at the pink egg next to his foot. "Really, here," he said, stooping to pick up the egg and handing it to the male officer.

He turned to the angry mansion owner. "I'm guessing these eggs are filled with more coins and treats?"

The coffee-wielding man shrugged. "Well, of course they are! It *is* Easter, after all."

Walt looked at the vast number of eggs surrounding them on the lawn and made a calculated decision.

"And I'm also guessing that most of the eggs with coins in them are full of nickels and dimes?"

The owner nodded.

"Well, of course. We have a budget and a grand prize that ate up most of that budget, and I saw you pick that up as well. You should be ashamed of yourself."

For the first time that morning, Walt smiled as he pointed to the pink egg.

"Well, I wasn't kidding! I was putting them back. I was going to replace everything when I realized the mistake I had made."

He paused. "And I'm really sorry about this... it was just one after the other, and it didn't dawn on me that this was..."

"Something planned?" inquired the male officer.

Walt nodded. "So please, open the pink egg. It has a quarter in it, not a nickel or dime. It's a shiny new quarter, and I'll even tell you the date on it if you promise not to arrest me."

He sighed. "I live just over three blocks away, and my family will be wondering what has happened to me."

The male officer pursed his lips and furrowed his brow. "Okay, maybe we arrest you and maybe not. So tell me, what's the date?"

Walt immediately said, "2020."

The homeowner hooted. "Oh, for crying out loud, they haven't even made 2020 quarters yet. Officers, take him away; I really need to go."

The female officer took out her handcuffs, stepped toward Walt, and began to recite the Miranda to him as the male officer opened the pink egg and inhaled loudly. He held the shiny coin out in front of him with an incredulous smile on his face and winked at Walt.

"It's a 2020 quarter. Sir, I guess you were mistaken."

He handed the quarter to the mansion owner.

The man looked at it. "That's impossible!"

Walt shrugged. "I told you so."

The female officer stepped back and replaced her handcuffs. "So you really were replacing the eggs and the coins."

Walt nodded vehemently.

The police officers looked over at the mansion owner. "Sir... it sure looks like he was doing exactly that. But if you insist, we can arrest him and throw him in jail. It's up to you."

Walt damn near fainted again.

The male officer stepped toward the owner, handing him the pink egg. "However, sir, the man was just out for a jog, and it seems he got a bit carried away." He hesitated. "After all, it is Easter, sir, and he is a neighbor of yours."

Hesitating again, he smiled his best cop smile. "If it were me, I'd let it go—no harm, no foul."

The owner hefted the runner's pouch and flung it over his shoulder.

"Do what you want, officers; I really need to get going."

Walt hung his head, then looked expectantly at the officers. "Am I free to go?"

The officers looked at each other and nodded. "Yes, sir, you are free to go."

Walt wasted no time—he ran to the fence and jumped over, sans running pouch, and headed down the sidewalk toward home sweet home.

A block later, Walt felt the police car tailing him and paused.

Oh my God, did they change their minds? he thought to himself. He considered speeding up and dashing down an alley—or something!

But he didn't... thank God.

As the police car slowly stopped next to him, Walt was signaled over by the male officer. He rolled down the passenger window and poked out his head. Smiling sympathetically, the officer stretched out his hand, which was holding a twenty-dollar bill.

He winked at Walt and whispered, "Have a happy Easter, sir."

The Marshal's First Father's Day

U.S. Deputy Marshal Barrett Frances Chisum set the bag of clean diapers and assorted baby items on the saloon counter and grinned at his brother, U.S. Deputy Beau Franklin Chisum.

His brother slapped him on the back and beckoned to the barkeep as he took a swig of his beer. The barkeep, a rotund, jovial man with the best handlebar mustache that Barrett had ever seen, reached across the bar and gave the marshal a firm handshake.

"Hey, Marshal, I haven't seen you since the wedding. Where have you been keeping yourself?"

Barrett grinned, pointing at the beer spigot. "I have been tying up loose ends," he said. He took off his badge and unbuckled his gun belt, handing them both to his brother, who grimaced but slid the badge into his front shirt pocket and set the gun and its holster on the bar.

"So, do you still have cold beer?" Barrett inquired.

The bartender shrugged. "Maybe, but it ain't cold and it ain't warm. More like it's *cool*, just like me." He slapped his knee and bellowed out a laugh.

Barrett held up two fingers.

"Get my brother one as well, since he is the one who's going to be carrying the badge from now on."

Beau chuckled softly as he finished the last of his beer and pushed the glass toward the bartender. He pulled the baby bag toward him and started removing its contents, holding up a baby pacifier.

"What the hell is this?" he asked, as the server set down the cool beers in front of the brothers.

Now it was Barrett's turn to chuckle.

"That is a newfangled invention called a baby comforter. It was invented by Christian Meinecke in 1901. They say it helps the baby to sleep, and by God, I'm going to try anything.

His brother nodded and handed the invention to his brother, who dipped it in his beer and promptly stuck it in his mouth.

Beau Chisum snorted. "Yeah, I heard little Frances is a bit colicky."

Just then, the saloon's batwing doors flew open and Frank Hancock Castillo pompously strode into the saloon, his hammer strap off. He stepped to the side of the door, taking the time to size up everyone in the joint. His gaze settled on the former Marshal Barrett Chisum, the baby comforter still in his mouth.

Frank shook his head in bewilderment. He strode to the far end of the bar and crooked his finger at the barkeep.

"Get me a bottle of your best whiskey," he said, slapping down a gold coin and staring at Barrett Chisum. "And get that man a baby bottle on my tab." He smirked and hesitated. "But I ain't going to change his diapers," he added, which made most of the bar patrons laugh—including the bartender.

Just not Barrett Frances Chisum.

•••••••••••••

Frank Hancock Castillo, taller than most men, had a chiseled, nearly handsome face, which was memorable because it bore a scar from over his left eye down to his chin. It was the result of a bar fight where he'd ended up the victor. His opponent had brought a knife to a gunfight and, as it turned out, it was the wrong choice of weapon. Frank, on the other hand, had no use for knives since he was considered a fast draw. And he had no back up in him at all—especially when he was drunk. Frank had killed his family when he was a teenager, and he'd been on a killing spree ever since. Mostly because he enjoyed it.

There was nothing criminal that he hadn't done. He had robbed trains and banks, and he had raped nearly two dozen women—some who went on to have his bastard children.

As the locals drank the cool beer, Frank took shot after shot of good whiskey, ignoring the bar crowd and fingering his scar absentmindedly. The bar began to clear out as the locals went home to their families and supper.

Barrett finished his beer, picked up the baby bag, slapped his brother on the shoulder, and began to push through the batwing doors. As he did so, a half-drunk Frank Castillo called out to him.

"Hey, baby, you headed home to get your diapers changed?"

The former marshal stopped and turned around slowly.

"Excuse me? Are you talking to me?" He stepped toward the criminal, handing the baby bag to the man nearest him.

Frank stepped away from the bar and looked around him.

"Yeah, I guess I am, baby girl."

Barrett looked at his brother, who nodded at the gun still lying on the bar as if to say, take it; it's yours.

Barrett hesitated.

He had promised his new bride that he would not carry a handgun once the baby was born and that he would quit working as a lawman and take a job in her father's tonsorial shop as an apprentice barber. The thought of it still made him shudder.

Barrett Frances Chisum was a Scotsman on his mother's side; her father had been a fair boxer and a renowned wrestler. According to legend, he had soundly defeated President Abraham Lincoln in a rough-and-tumble match on the White House lawn. And he had taught Beau and Barrett everything he knew, including all of his dirty tricks.

Even without a gun as a weapon, Barrett was fully prepared to give the half-drunk Frank Castillo a run for his money.

As he moved toward Frank with a deep growl, Frank did the unexpected, slicking his smoke wagon out, pointing it at Barrett, and beginning to pull the trigger. And just as quickly, Beau stepped in front of his unarmed brother, his Colt appearing out of nowhere as he pulled back the hammer. Frank hesitated, hearing other guns being cocked around him—and stopped cold when he heard the ratchet of a 12-gauge shotgun and a voice behind him that calmly said, "Let me have 'im, Beau, I'll blow his darn head off!"

Frank tilted his gun toward the floor and looked around. Every man was pointing some sort of gun at him, from pistols to rifles to shotguns. Barrett took a step forward, snatched Frank's gun out of his hand, and pointed it at him. Then he flipped it over and handed it to his brother handle-first.

Barrett smiled and chuckled.

"Okay, Mr. Drifter, how about if this baby girl gives you the beating of your life?" He headbutted Frank, then dove at his legs, and suddenly Frank was on Barrett's shoulders, spinning around wildly.

Barrett threw open the saloon's batwing doors and tossed Frank Hancock Castillo out into the dusty street, following right behind as he stripped off his long-sleeved shirt, revealing his long, rock-hard muscles. A dizzy Frank staggered to get up as Barrett shot toward him for a single-leg take-down. The still-dizzy Frank ended up in the street with Barrett on top of him, his forearm under Frank's chin, pushing hard on his windpipe. Frank gasped for breath, then started to black out, his eyes rolling over into the back of his head.

Barrett stood up and his brother handed him a glass of beer, which he gratefully took, downing it quickly.

The man holding the baby bag pulled it open, motioning for a few of his friends. They proceeded to pull the pants off Frank's, laughing and snickering as they diapered the unconscious man with a half-dozen diapers. The bartender led Frank's horse over to the diaper gang and the three men boosted him up into the saddle and tied him down. The barkeep, now standing on the boardwalk, stuck the baby comforter in Frank's mouth and shut it with adhesive tape. The livery owner handed a half-full bucket of tar to the barkeep and laughed uproariously as he dumped it over the back of Frank's head and upper torso.

Beau Chisum mounted his horse and led Frank down the main street as the locals jeered and tossed anything handy at him—including eggs, both fresh and rotten. A soiled dove who had suffered Frank's wrath earlier in the day and had not been paid rushed out onto the boardwalk with a feather pillow cut open on one end, gleefully dumping it over the outlaw's head. The citizens cheered and the prostitute curtsied.

Beau rode till it was nearly dark, then stopped and dropped the horse's reins. Then he pulled out his Colt and pointed it at the now wide-awake Frank Castillo, his eyes wide as saucers and his body shaking with fright. Beau tapped his U.S. deputy marshal badge and smiled benevolently at Frank.

"Now, that baby girl that you just got wiped by is my little brother, and he is also a U.S. deputy marshal."

He paused, pursing his lips, his brow furrowed.

"I don't need to tell you what happens to a man that kills or injures a U.S. marshal, and if you don't already know, you really don't want to," he said, making a hanging gesture.

"So I don't ever want to see you in these parts again—in fact, stay the hell out of Texas."

Beau turned his horse, then stopped.

"Say, is your sorry ass a father?"

Frank mumbled a yes through the baby pacifier, thinking of all the women he had raped in his life.

Beau laughed out loud. "Wouldn't you know it? Goddamn wonders never cease." He turned back toward town and trotted off, calling back over his shoulder, "HAPPY FA-THER'S DAY!

Just Another Morning

Diane heard a strange sort of whomping noise that she had never heard before—an alien sound that seemed to belong on another planet.

Whomp.

And the World Trade Center shook as if it were attempting to dance.

She looked outside to see a piece of something fall past her window, then another, then another. She rose tentatively and grabbed her crutch. The full cast on her leg was almost new, with only three signatures on the white fiberglass. She smiled at the picture that a young neighbor had drawn—a smiley face with its tongue hanging out and the words "god luk Diane" written underneath.

She kept smiling… right until her foot hit the floor.

Ouch. Ouch. Ouch.

She regretted letting her fiancé William talk her into going skiing at Lake Tahoe. "Just a getaway before the wedding. It'll be good for us," he'd said.

"Good for us, my ass," she mumbled, making her way over to the office window, which was filling up with her coworkers.

Her boss, Peter, was pointing at people on the sidewalk. As another large piece of something fell, the pedestrians turned and ran for their lives.

Peter sniffed. "I smell diesel." Then he stopped talking and gasped. "Oh my God, that's jet fuel!"

Peter had enough frequent flyer miles to circle the earth. If he said it was jet fuel, Diane believed him.

The woman next to Peter started coughing, and then the man next to Diane did the same. Diane's good friend Amanda starting coughing too, then grabbed her wastebasket and threw up into it. Now, the whole office smelled of jet fuel and vomit. *Nice.*

Then someone pointed at the television in the corner, which had been switched from talking heads and their takes on the current market to a shot of the World Trade Center.

Someone cranked the volume up.

"It appears that a large airplane has hit the World Trade Center. We have no information on whether it was an accident or deliberate." The newsreader paused, then shook his head in disbelief. "We have now confirmed that a second plane has hit the other tower." He shuddered visibly. "Apparently, this is not an accident. It appears that the World Trade Center is under attack!"

Amanda fell to the ground in a dead faint. An outer door opened, and a man in a maintenance uniform shouted,

"The elevators aren't working! Everyone needs to use the stairs, and hurry!" He left as the overwhelming smell of smoke joined the scents of fuel and vomit.

People were frozen in place watching the television, and then someone pointed out that the offices where they were now standing were about fifteen stories below the point of impact.

Peter jumped up on a vacant desk. "Everyone, stay calm. We need to move into the hall and go to the stairway. We don't have much time, so take your phone and nothing else. No personal computers, no briefcases or files. I need the women to go first. Now, let's move."

Then he snapped off the television. He looked at Diane with her cast and crutch. "Di, why don't you wait with me. We can bring up the rear. I'll help you."

Diane nodded and took one last look out the window. Fire trucks, ambulances, and police cars were pulling up in front of the towers while all of the pedestrians were running in the opposite direction. "Incredible," she whispered to herself before turning and leaving the office.

Peter exited his office with a laptop in hand, and Diane gave him a dirty look.

"I know, I know, but if this office goes up in smoke, what I have on this laptop will save the firm. I hope," Peter explained. He opened the door, and the building shook again as if possessed.

Diane stepped out into the hall, a bit miffed that Peter was holding on to his precious computer rather than helping her as promised. The long hall was starting to fill with smoke, and she crutched her way down to the door to the stairway with Peter right on her tail.

As she reached out to open the door, she turned to her boss. "Damn it, Peter, I'm frightened."

Peter smiled. "Yeah, me too, Di. I guess that must mean we're human. Let's get the hell out of here!"

Diane threw open the door without any idea of what she would find behind it. What she saw was that the stairwell was packed with people heading down to safety. As they streamed slowly by, she recognized a few she'd seen in the cafeteria, but no one she'd ever spoken to. "I guess it's too late to get to know them now," she mumbled to herself. Her heel hit the top stair, and pain radiated up her leg.

Peter stepped in front of her and stopped the flow of people. "Hold on, folks. We have an injured lady here. Just hold on."

Diane pursed her lips and nodded in gratitude, then seized the handrail and joined the descending crowd with Peter following right behind her. The stairs were narrow, and Diane was slowed by her leg and her crutch, so the people streamed around her. Some offered words of encouragement and some made nasty remarks, like "Get out of the way, bitch!"

Three floors down, the right side of the stairway was

suddenly filled with emergency personnel. First came four policemen headed up to who knows where. Then a paramedic crew blew by, wearing scared but determined expressions. They were followed by a unit of firefighters wearing helmets and backpacks, and some were carrying axes. As Diane slowly made her way down the stairs in excruciating pain, she marveled at them. They had the same look of determination as the paramedics, but from the expressions on their young faces, it seemed as if they weren't frightened at all.

Hell, they looked like they were going to spend the afternoon at the beach.

With the new two-way traffic, Diane heard more rude mumbles behind her.

"Goddamn it, hurry up!"

"What's the hold up?"

"Damn it, we're going to die!" someone screeched.

Exhausted and in pain, Diane stopped at the next landing and wedged herself into the corner. Peter crowded in beside her, and she laughed to herself when she recognized the smell of his aftershave.

"Di, why are we stopping? We need to keep going!"

She touched her boss's shoulder. "You keep going. I just need a bit of a rest."

"I'm staying with you."

A woman bumped him on the side. "Move over, mister! You're blocking the way."

Peter moved in tighter, and Diane chuckled nervously. "If you get any closer, we're going to have children."

"Come on, Di, let's keep going. I'm blocking the aisle."

She put her foot down and the pain surged up her leg again. "Not now. You go on without me. I'll be down shortly." She cupped her hand behind her boss's neck and gave him a kiss on the cheek. "And if I'm not, give William a hug and a kiss and tell him that he was the love of my life. I'll be right behind you. Go check on the rest of our workers."

Peter nodded and stroked her cheek.

Then he was gone.

Diane backed farther into the small corner on the landing, and it was as if she had disappeared. The occupants of the tower moved past her, some on cell phones, some talking to those in front or behind. One person was even trying to text as he made his way down the stairway and kept bumping into the person in front of him.

Unbelievable, she thought.

Most of the tower's occupants were quiet. Many had a look of calm, as if they were stuck in a bad dream and this would all be over when their alarm went off. Others were mumbling prayers under their breath, and a few had a look of real concern on their faces.

Actually, more than a few.

The line halted momentarily when a woman stopped and gripped Diane's elbow. She was an elderly, petite African American. She smiled at Di. "Hey, girl, what'cha doin' in the corner? Come on, we need to get you out of here." She spoke as calmly as if they were going out for a stroll in the rain.

Diane smiled at her just as the next man in line pushed the woman forward. "Come on, get the fuck out of the way!"

The tiny woman flew down the stairs, screaming at the man behind her. Over her shoulder, she gave Diane a look of exasperation, and then she vanished around the corner.

Diane sighed and stayed put.

•••••••••••••

Fire Chief Tad Pennington normally did not lead his firefighters into a building. But this burning tower situation was not normal, so he was doing so now, taking a dozen men up the stairway past the tower's occupants, who were streaming out to safety. A few of them even gave his men encouraging words. For the most part, though, they simply hurried to get out of harm's way.

After more than forty years as a firefighter, the chief was

planning to retire the week before Thanksgiving. He was a large man, still muscular and fit at the age of sixty, and his physique served him well. As he marched his squad up one narrow flight of stairs after another, his sons followed right behind: Tad Jr., an experienced firefighter, and his youngest, Nate, a second-year fireman who was catching on quickly. As strong as an ox, Nate had always bested all of the other men in the station in their weekly weightlifting competitions. He had two young children and a beautiful wife who was currently pregnant with their third child.

Chief Pennington turned a corner and spotted a woman wedged into the corner of the landing. She had a full-length cast on her leg and a crutch next to her and was obviously in pain. He stopped when he reached her and held up a hand to stem the flow of people. Then he took off his helmet and smiled at her.

"Hello, ma'am. How's your morning going so far?" he asked with a straight face.

She burst into laughter, then tears. "Not so well. But you're headed in the wrong direction, sir."

The chief shook his head. "Well, I'm not sure about that. And what are you doing here? You need to get to safety."

The woman gestured at the other workers of the World Trade Center, who were getting impatient and hollering nasty things at them. "I was holding up the crowd, so I stopped to catch my breath. I haven't seen an opening to start moving again." The building shuddered again, and several people screamed.

Chief Pennington looked down at his youngest son. "Nate, take this woman outside. Don't leave her alone. Take care of her—and don't think about coming back in. We'll be just fine, and we'll be out soon."

Nate grimaced at the thought of leaving his father, his brother, and his buddies, but he nodded. "Yes, sir."

With that, the chief moved up and away, and Nate took his place in front of Diane. "Here, get on my back, like a piggy-back ride." Diane climbed up with help, and Nate started downward, to the relief of the tower residents backed up behind him.

As they began moving, Diane called over her shoulder, "Be safe, Chief!"

The chief continued to lead his men up and not down, chuckling at Diane's parting words.

"I'll try."

••••••••••••

Nate and Diane made their way down the long staircase and into the lobby, finally pushing outside through the revolving doors just as the tower collapsed.

Nate wasted no time, adjusting his human cargo and hurrying as quickly as possible down the street. The crunch of the litter on the pavement reverberated through his boots and up his legs. The other pedestrians were either turning and running or glued to the sidewalk as if they could not believe what was happening in front of them. As the towers pancaked, a huge cloud of dust and ash followed them—an evil, man-made sandstorm.

Panicked New Yorkers rushed away from the fallen building. The street became a cacophony of people's screams and wails as they hurried to get out of harm's way, their cell phones all but forgotten.

Nate rushed past abandoned taxis and cars as sirens of all sorts filled the dusty air. As the dust storm engulfed the couple, Diane was caught in a hacking cough, and Nate began to slow down.

He turned at the next corner. Both of them were now covered with dust, their faces as white as mimes.

Nate stopped, exhausted. Diane wiggled off his back as Nate slumped down against a brick wall. Diane looked down at her rescuer and did the same, her cast out to one side.

She gripped his forearm, thinking, *Thank you, Nate. Thank you so much.*

Nate sucked in a mouthful of air and dust and began to cough. He wept silently at first, then louder and louder. He began to shudder as he removed his ash-covered fire helmet and placed it gently on his lap, as if it were a sacred relic. He bent forward and sobbed as if there was no tomorrow, and Diane put her arms around his back in a reverse hug, squeezing as tightly as she could.

"I'm so sorry," she told him. "It's going to be okay."

And then they both cried and cried and cried.

Epilogue

Diane and Nate's families grew close after their shared experience. Chief Pennington and his crew were among the 343 firefighters who did not return to safety from the twin towers.

It was not long before Nate's wife, Rebecca, gave birth to fraternal twins. The boy was named Tad, of course, and the beautiful girl was named Diane.

The Birthday Gift

Nature was calling… urgently. Chris was standing in a long line in the bathroom at Target Field. Just as he approached the urinal, the scene changed and he found himself walking up and down a hallway, pounding on every door and begging to use the bathroom. The next thing he knew, he was stuck in traffic, holding his legs together and trying desperately not to wet himself. Suddenly, he smelled coffee brewing. He was standing in the doorway to his kitchen and his brother Kirk was sitting at the counter, sipping from a steaming cup.

"Hey bro, hope you don't mind I made myself some coffee." Kirk smiled. "Help yourself."

Chris froze. "Kirk, what the heck are you doing here? You… you're gone."

"Yeah, I know, I'm dead." Kirk grinned. "But as you no doubt remember, today's my birthday and the good Lord lets everyone come back to Earth on their birthday to visit one special person for twenty-four hours. I thought about visiting Mom but it would only confuse her. And besides, your coffee is a lot better than hers. So here I am!"

Chris walked over to the coffee maker and poured himself a cup. He sat down at the kitchen table, shaking his head in amazement. "So are you a ghost?"

"No way!" Kirk extended a hand to Chris. "Here, feel this. I'm flesh and bone, just like you."

Chris set his coffee cup on the table and tentatively shook Kirk's hand. And by God, he was right. Kirk's hand was warm and muscular, with the same familiar grip.

Unbelievable, Chris thought to himself. Kirk got up from his barstool and refilled his mug. "I gotta say, heaven's a decent place but believe it or not, you can't get a good cup of java there to save your life." He sat down next to Chris and picked up a book. "Rescued by Chris Fleischauer," he read aloud. "Hey bro, you've been busy since I left. I just finished reading it and I'm impressed. It's a pretty damn good Western!"

"Whaddya mean you just finished it?" Chris said incredulously. "How long have you been here?"

Kirk grinned. "Since midnight. And now that I know you're writing Westerns, I'll ask the library in heaven to stock them. I'm sure they'll say yes, since there's no porn."

Chris put his hand on Kirk's shoulder. "I've gotta be honest, little bro. I'm finding this all a little hard to believe."

"It's the God's honest truth," he grinned. "Oh, and by the way, Dad says hello. He's busy playing sheepshead with God and John Wayne. God told Dad he likes sheepshead because he's tired of poker and he won't play bridge with the nuns because they cheat."

"Who knew God was a card shark?" Chris laughed and shook his head.

"Hey, remember when we were kids and we walked through Iverson Park and there was that car full of teenagers who yelled nasty things at us? It was so awesome. I'll never forget the way you ran over to the car, pulled the guy through the passenger window, and punched him right in the nose!"

"Yeah, that was not my finest moment." Chris grimaced at the memory.

"You were a total rock star," Kirk continued. "And remember when I was little and Tim Murray kidnapped me and put me in their family's dog kennel? Man, did that stink! And then you rode up the driveway on your green bike, let me out, and gave Tim all kinds of hell."

Chris smiled. "Yeah, I guess I did okay. At least I didn't punch Tim in the nose."

"You're the best," Kirk said fondly. "Hey, how about a pizza? I'm hungry." Chris nodded and picked up his phone. He called their favorite pizza place and ordered a large pepperoni. They broke open a couple of beers and recounted more stories from their childhood while they waited for the pizza to be delivered.

It was nearing midnight when Kirk stood up and took one last swallow of his beer. "Hey bro, I've gotta go. I don't want to get locked out of the pearly gates." He punched Chris in the shoulder and walked towards the front door.

"Ouch!" Chris rubbed his arm as he followed Kirk down the hall.

"Oh, come on now, that's just something to remember me by." Kirk gave Chris a long hug. He opened the door, revealing a giant, pumpkin-colored moon.

"Boy, do I miss my family and this glorious Earth," Kirk sighed to himself. He turned back towards Chris with a smirk. "Hey, by the way, big brother, don't you still need to pee?"

Chris sat up in his bed with a start. Kirk was right. He really needed to pee. He threw his legs over the side of the bed and headed for the bathroom to relieve himself. As he washed his hands, he caught his reflection in the mirror.

"Son of a gun!" he said, looking down at a dark purple bruise on his shoulder.

"I'll get you next year, little brother."

The Chalice

The men met in a support group sponsored by the Survivors Network of Those Abused by Catholic Priests—otherwise known simply as "the Network."

Each man in the group had been abused at the hands of a Catholic priest known as Father Franklin Recker, whose last name was appropriate because he made it a habit of wrecking young men's lives.

He was now defrocked.

Finally.

Many years ago, the group had first met in the basement of a cold and damp Baptist church that smelled of mold and dead mice. Lots of dead mice.

And perhaps, because they were all victims of the same priest (or because they were all about the same age, or maybe because they were all poker players), they bonded and became good friends.

So now they were together in Ted Wilson's living room, playing a game of five-card stud. Two of the poker players were smoking cigars, three were drinking beer, and Fritz, who had been the most devout Catholic of them all prior to being abused by the above-mentioned pedophile priest, was doing neither of the two. His passion centered around his three beautiful golden retrievers, Jake, Sophie, and Rusty. Rusty had been nicknamed "Treat" because he lived for treats.

Fritz was also a darn good poker player.

And as a result of his abstinence from the alcohol, he was, in fact, winning—rather substantially.

Ted, the host, dejectedly tossed his cards into the middle of the table and rubbed the back of his head. He took a ferocious puff of his cigar, blowing foul-smelling smoke rings at the yellowed and water-stained ceiling.

"Fritz, how the hell can you be so good?" Ted asked as he pursed his lips into a scowl, watching his smoke spread out. "I'm thinking you must be cheating.'

The card players froze in silence. They could have heard an ant fart.

Fritz looked across the table and calmly considered the frustrated Ted. He pulled his hand out from underneath the table and pointed a gun at the other man... or rather, his fingers in the shape of a gun.

"You know, my friend, in the Old West, you could get shot for saying such a thing," Fritz answered.

Then he pulled the imaginary trigger.

POW!

Holding his index finger up to his mouth, Fritz mimicked blowing smoke off the end of the pistol, then reached for his water and chuckled quietly.

Brian, who was sitting next to Fritz, flung his cards at Ted, nearly hitting the flaming tip of his cigar. "Are you nuts, Ted?" he demanded. "Fritz cheating, my ass! You haven't been paying attention to the game since we sat down. I've never seen you play so poorly. I'm guessing you have something on your mind."

The fourth player, Antwan Bakhtiari, the only African American in the group, took the last swallow from his Guinness Stout with a small lemon wedge stuck inside the bottle and intentionally belched loudly.

It broke the mood, and Antwan continued Brian's thoughts. "First of all, gentlemen, no one is cheating. Fritz is just a better player than us. He's been carrying us for a long time. If he wanted, he could've cleaned us out years ago."

He paused and pushed his cards slowly and deliberately toward the middle of the beer-stained poker table. "But Brian is right. Ted, my friend, you have something on your mind, don't you? So either spit it out or go get me another damn beer."

Then he leaned toward Ted and belched again. It was a bit quieter and accompanied by a wink this time.

Ted shook his head good-naturedly, waving the smell of the belch away from his face. Standing up to go to the kitchen, he called over his shoulder, "Yeah, you're right. I'll fetch more beer and tell you what I'm thinking."

•••••••••••••

Fritz sipped his water and gazed at the two remaining card players. At this point in his life, they were his best friends. They got together over the poker table on a regular basis and shared stories of both the good and the bad that had happened to them since they last met.

Brian was the only one of the four who was gay, and he also was the only one who was married to a life partner. He was a reserved sort of fellow, an actuary by profession. He was rumored to be good at hacking into computers and data-bases. Furthermore, Brian was probably the best poker player at the table, but he played too conservatively, and he had a tell: when he had a great hand, his right eye twitched.

Fritz took advantage of this, especially when the pot was large.

Antwan, on the other hand, was a different story. He was *definitely* not gay. He was a single, straight male with ex-otic indigo eyes and skin as black as the ace of spades.

And Antwan was a ladies' man.

He was film-star handsome, but with one blemish: he had a patch of white vitiligo on his chin that ran to the start of his neck.

The women loved it. Go figure.

Furthermore, he was the group's hero.

Once, after Father Franklin Recker had been drummed out of the church, the former priest was visiting a few of his remaining friends in Florida. Coincidently—or not—he was staying near Antwan's parents' condo on Sanibel Island. He had the audacity to call Antwan's parents to invite them to dinner. Not that he ever paid—it was much more likely that he would not only ask the couple to pay, but also ask them for money.

When Antwan had answered the phone, he'd used the unexpected opportunity well.

Antwan was alone at the condo for a week, using the small gym and biking to get into shape and possibly make the acquaintance of some Southern belles. So when he picked up the phone and realized who he was talking to, he was stunned. His scalp felt as if it was crawling with pedophilic lice.

But he recovered quickly.

Especially when Recker finally realized that it was Antwan on the other end of the line and uttered the same creepy phrase he'd used twenty years before, hissing, "Are you alone in the house?"

And Antwan damn near lost it.

Almost.

With bile rising into his throat and the smell of vomit in his sinuses, he responded, "Yes, I am alone, Father."

"How about if I come over and we get reacquainted?" Recker purred into the phone. "I'm just down the block at Starbucks."

Forcing himself to swallow the bile, Antwan said, "Sure, why not?"

He quickly hung up.

Twenty-five minutes later, a knock sounded on the door. Antwan opened it, and there stood his childhood adversary. The man had aged poorly. He had dark bags under his lascivious eyes and was greedily drinking in the image of the fit, athletic Antwan.

The former priest started to step forward to give Antwan a hug, but Antwan quickly put out his arm to stop him. "I'll be goddamned, if it isn't Franklin fucking Recker. Long time no see."

Antwan then furrowed his brow and squinted at the defrocked priest, nearly closing his eyes as disgusting, decades-old images flashed through his mind.

Standing there with the door open, Antwan sucked in his breath, trying to stay in the present. He'd been waiting for this moment for well over twenty years. He wanted to savor it.

In doing so, he noticed the sweet smell of the azalea bushes next to him as well as the pungent scent of the newly mowed lawn that stretched out behind the eager pedophile. He exhaled, still in the moment. He glanced up at the baking Florida sun as it poured out its oranges and reds into the horizon like a cauldron of molten lava.

He started to smile.

Then he punched the asshole right in his bulbous, red-veined, alcoholic nose.

As the former priest held his crimson-gushing schnoz, Antwan proceeded to give the man a dressing down for the ages. He ripped the pedophile a proverbial new asshole, dumping out decades of pent-up anger. His tirade was spiced with nearly every swear word that Antwan knew. He concluded his wrathful outburst with what would happen to the priest if he didn't stay away from Antwan's parents.

Then he slammed the door shut for good measure.

Clunk!

And he damn near giggled with relief.

•••••••••••••

Ted returned from the kitchen with three more beers, a Diet Coke instead of water for Fritz, and quite the interesting story.

Apparently, one of the Jackson and Jackson family, owners of the huge international corporation whose headquarters were located just outside of Milwaukee, had recently passed and had left the Catholic Church quite a bequest. The late Richard Jackson had been a devoted churchgoer and had been collecting chalices his entire life, some of them worth a king's ransom. And he was offering the church the pick of ten of them.

According to the newspaper article, they were going to be viewed by Milwaukee Archbishop Cousins at Jackson's home next Saturday evening.

Ted's plan was ingenious, kind of.

The poker crew would dress as two bishops and two priests and arrive mid-afternoon at the Jackson home, posing as Archbishop Cousins and another bishop, one who was an expert on chalices. They would call the home and confirm that the widow would be there, suggesting that perhaps they might arrive early.

As Ted finished his tale, he looked around at the group. His friends were lost in thought, so Ted finished, "What do you think?"

It was Brian who spoke up first. "You know, we've watched lots of victims of these damn priests get astronomical pay-outs in other states. But we all know it's not going to happen in ours. And it might be nice to get rewarded for the pain and agony we've been through."

He chuckled quietly. "Hell, between the four of us, we've probably spent over fifty thousand dollars on shrinks!"

The rest of the men nodded in complete agreement.

It was Antwan who spoke next. "I agree with that, and it would be nice to get something back... but Ted, your plan seems kind of sketchy. And what's the goal? Do we steal all of the chalices, or only a few of them? And what if the widow gets wise and calls the Archbishop ahead of time, and the police are there when we show up?"

Ted sighed wearily, his shoulders dropping in disappointment. "Then we're screwed," he replied.

Brian took a swig of his cold beer and cleared his throat. "On the other hand, who calls people, especially an Archbishop? I'm guessing they're emailing the Bishop—or one of his representatives."

Ted puffed on his cigar and blew the nasty-smelling smoke at the ceiling. It formed a huge smoke ring that the group paused to watch until it hit the yellowed ceiling and dissipated.

Ted turned to Brian. "Good point, Brian. So what do you propose?"

Brian grinned and wiggled his eyebrows like Groucho Marx. "Well, I can hack into their computers... as long as they have wireless."

Antwan sipped his dark beer and leaned forward. "Everyone has wireless, so I'm sure these people do. I mean, they're zillionaires." He pointed his beer bottle at Brian. "But we can sit just down the block from their house to make sure."

He paused and frowned. "But what about passwords?"

They all regarded Brian as he smiled a sinful smile. "Oh, don't worry about that."

•••••••••••••

Brian and Fritz had parked a block over from the late Richard Jackson's house, which was actually a huge brick mansion. They were delighted to find that it did, in fact, have Wi-Fi.

So Brian wasted no time. He keyed in a password, and it didn't work.

He tried another.

And another.

Then he let out a deafening primal scream. "I'm in!"

Fritz covered his ears as he shook his head in amazement. "How the hell did you do that?"

Brian looked up from his sleek personal computer and winked at him. "Well, my man... I looked up the widow on the Internet. She's really good looking, and lo and behold, she has red hair."

He smirked. "Really, really red hair."

He paused, glancing up at Fritz. "So I entered the password *RuthRed* first. Then I tried *RedRuth* and finally *RuthRedhead*, and that did it."

He started to hack into the redheaded widow's email as he continued his password lecture. "The most common password is a person's birthday and their initials, maybe with a special character added. The character is normally an exclamation point. So if her birthday is 02-24-1978, her password might be RJ02241978! Or some variation of that, and Richard apparently robbed the cradle since she is much younger than him. But redheads are different: redheads take pride in their hair, especially women. So their passwords always—and I mean *always*—have something to do with red hair."

He smirked. "I listened to a password lecture on it few years ago. The lecturer was, of course, a redheaded woman."

Still working on the computer, he pursed his lips, making his cavernous dimples stand out. Then he whooped again—slightly more quietly this time.

"What? What is it?" enquired Fritz.

"Red is communicating with a priest named Taylor Fitzpatrick, and he's apparently excited about the generous gift. The priest has confirmed the Saturday evening appointment at her home, and the Archbishop will be in attendance as well."

Fritz rocked back and forth on his ample buttocks with a mischievous sneer on his face. "Excellent," he said as Brian's fingers flew rapidly across the keyboard.

Brian was typing a reply to the redheaded widow.

Dear Ruth,

We are so looking forward to meeting you on Saturday. All of us in the diocese appreciate you and your late husband's generosity. May he rest in peace.

We would like you to know that Archbishop Cousins would like to hold a mass in his honor at a later date and that you and your family will be the guests of honor.

But in regard to Saturday, we will be bringing an expert on chalices, a bishop from the East Coast. As a result, we would like to move the appointment up by a few hours, as he needs to return that evening. If that is acceptable, we will arrive promptly at 3 p.m.

Sincerely,

Taylor Fitzpatrick JCL

Fritz started the car and headed back toward Ted's place.

"Rest in peace... nice touch. So while he is *resting*, she is free to do anything. If she is as young and good looking as you described, maybe when this is all over, I can ask her out on a date."

Brian shook his head and turned into the street. "That's terrible. How could you even think of such a thing?" he asked with a scowl.

Fritz laughed out loud.

"Hey, I'm just sayin'."

•••••••••••••

Ted hung up his landline with a smile on his face. "My uncle says we can use one of his limos as long as Fritz is driving. I told him we were bar hopping on Saturday, and he knows Fritz doesn't drink."

Fritz looked up from his computer. "Dang, I wanted to be the East Coast bishop."

"With that ugly mutt of a face, I don't think so," Antwan sneered. "You're Midwest all the way."

Fritz smiled a saintly smile and hit a key on his computer to bring up priest costumes on Amazon. He picked out one for himself, then looked at the rest of his buddies. "Okay, who's going to be the other priest?"

Brian raised his hand. "That would be me. After all, I am gay and handsome as hell."

As everyone laughed, Fritz glanced at Brian. "What size are you, medium?"

Brian nodded, and Fritz ordered the priest costumes with a simple keystroke. Then he moved to another Amazon page for bishop clothing and examined Ted.

"Okay, Ted my pal, do you want to be the East Coast bishop or Archbishop Cousins?"

"He needs to be Archbishop Cousins," Antwan interrupted. "After all, the real bishop is white. So I'll be the other bishop, maybe a Boston bishop?" He did a nice imitation of a Boston accent.

Fritz hit the order key for a large bishop costume and chortled. "You have to love Amazon—they'll be here on Thursday."

•••••••••••••

Saturday came quickly, and the nattily dressed faux clergy began to pile into the limousine. Antwan was wearing a long beard to cover his vitiligo, and he also sported a fake ruby red cubic zirconia bishop's ring. Again, thanks to Amazon, on sale for sixty-nine dollars. Antwan thought it complemented his red sash nicely.

Before he got in the stretch limo, Antwan strutted around on the sidewalk in his black bishop costume with the crimson sash around his waist, doing the backward Michael Jackson moonwalk and singing the song *Chalice* by Donae'O.

Fritz simply rolled his eyes at Antwan, thinking he looked more like a Russian Orthodox bishop with his long beard than an American one. As Fritz climbed into the driver's seat, he tugged at the uncomfortable priest's collar. He never wore a tie, even when he went to a funeral, and having the collar around his throat made him want to gag.

Brian sat next to him in the passenger's seat and glanced at himself in the rearview mirror. He smiled a priestly smile, thinking that he looked pretty good in the long robes. And he actually liked the bright white priest's collar. He thought it gave him a debonair look. He also had shaved his goatee, donned eyeglasses, and dyed his hair temporarily.

Ted sat behind Fritz and had brought a pack of cigarettes along. Not that he smoked cigarettes, but he thought that if someone from the house came out to check on him in the car, he might as well be smoking while he was on the phone. After all, it was well known that the Milwaukee bishop was a three-pack-a-day man, as well as a lover of bourbon.

Finally done with his moonwalk, Antwan got into the limo and closed the door, and Fritz headed across town to the mansion.

Fritz stayed in the right lane, keeping his speed just under the limit. There was no sense in getting busted by getting a ticket. The limo was a shiny new stretch limousine, and all of the passengers in the cars rolling past it tried to get a glimpse of the occupants. But the windows were heavily tinted, so they could only guess.

Before he pulled up to the Jackson mansion, Fritz circled the block to ensure there were no police cars in the vicinity.

There weren't.

So Fritz turned into the long paved driveway and pulled up to the front of the home. Fritz put the car in park, but made no move to get out. Ted lit up a cigarette and took out his cell phone as Brian and Antwan got out of the car and headed up to the door.

Brian went first, and he was about to ring the doorbell when the door opened. A lovely redheaded woman smiled at the clergymen gathered on her front stoop. She reached out her hand for a shake and asked Brian, "You must be Father Fitzpatrick?"

Brian did not miss a beat. "Yes, I am, but please call me Taylor or Father Taylor."

Then Antwan held out his hand for a shake—but the red-headed widow took his hand and half-curtsied over it, kissing Antwan's bishop's ring.

"Welcome, Bishop," she said. "It's an honor to have you in our humble home."

She looked over at the limo and tentatively waved at the tinted windows. "Isn't Bishop Cousins coming in?"

Brian frowned. "Perhaps, but he just got a call from the Vatican." He paused. "I believe it was the pope himself," he added in a whisper.

"Oh my!" exclaimed Ruth. "How exciting!"

She waved them into her lovely mansion and nimbly led them up a winding staircase. The counterfeit clergymen followed her into what might be described as a chalice and cross or crucifix room at the back of the house. One wall was filled with crosses, some beautiful and some very plain. There was a plaque under each that told a bit about its origins.

However, the majority of the room was filled with chalices, scores of chalices. Some were silver, some bronze, and some solid gold.

But what really caught Brian's and Antwan's attention was a lone chalice sitting on top of a small, shiny, waist-high mahogany table.

This chalice was breathtaking.

It was smaller than the rest of the chalices and appeared to be made of solid gold. It had a gold stem with a Latin phrase engraved on it: *Iesus Christus Natus Est.*

"Christ is risen."

The outside of the chalice was festooned with dazzling rubies just below its oversized lip, and below them were three rows of diamonds that glowed incandescently in the light. Finally, underneath it all, was a row of gleaming emeralds that seemed to beckon to the men, saying, "Come, pick me up and drink."

Antwan stepped toward the masterpiece, his eyes open as wide as a deer's in car headlights. He bent down to examine the chalice a bit more closely and was surprised to smell a delightful lemony aroma. Apparently, the mahogany table had been waxed recently with a lemon spray.

He inhaled the citrus aroma deeply before he stood up and turned toward the widow, thinking that it made sense: Jackson Wax had been the very first product of the successful company.

Antwan turned toward the beautiful widow. "This is magnificent. Do you mind if I ask how you and your late husband acquired it?"

The widow regarded the fake bishop. "We don't know its origins, but it was confiscated by the Nazis during World War II. I'm told that it was one of Himmler's favorites, and he drank champagne out of it on special occasions. When the war was over, it was smuggled out of Germany by an American soldier who held on to it, not wanting to sell or auction it for fear it would be taken from him. When he died, it was discovered in his attic by his daughter and was put up for auction on an invitation-only basis. Only six bidders were invited, and Richard actually outbid the Rockefellers for it."

She paused. "If you select this piece, then the offer for more chalices will no longer be valid. It is by far the most valuable piece and was appraised a decade ago for over ten million dollars."

Antwan and Brian sucked in their breath.

Antwan moved back toward the astonishing trophy, glancing at Ruth.

"May I pick it up?"

"By all means. After all, if you select it, it will belong to the church."

Antwan gently picked the chalice up and carefully walked over to the window, holding it up to the radiant autumn sun streaming through the glass. The sun reflected off of the jewels, and Antwan felt the hair on the back of his head stand up and salute.

By God, it was the most beautiful thing he had ever seen.

He gingerly put the chalice back down on the lemony table and nodded at the woman.

"Well, I would like to have it appraised, but if what you say is true—and I certainly have no reason to doubt you—the Church will be overjoyed to accept this in lieu of the other chalices."

He hesitated. "Would you mind if we take it with us for an appraisal?"

Ruth Jackson nodded again. "Please do. I will have our butler pack it up for you."

She turned and left the room, calling for her butler Albert.

Brian eyed Antwan and shivered.

"Holy cow, we hit the jackpot!"

•••••••••••••

Albert wrapped the magnificent chalice while Brian took pictures of the rest of the chalices with his cell phone, just in case. Ruth Jackson glanced at Brian as he was doing so.

"Isn't Bishop Cousins coming up?"

Brian took one last picture.

"He certainly planned to, but you don't really hang up on the pope."

"Well, of course not, but I haven't seen him in a few months, and I thought I could get his blessing."

Brian nodded at Antwan. He nearly said, "Bishop Antwan," but instead pulled a name out of the blue. "Bishop Scarmuzzo will be happy to bless you."

As Albert returned with the chalice, Bishop Antwan Scarmuzzo moved away from his examination of the wall of crosses and smiled his most pious smile at the widow. He glanced at Brian and gestured toward the door.

"I would be honored. Perhaps we could be left alone?"

Brian followed Albert out of the room.

At that point, Ruth Jackson dropped to her knees and began to weep silently. "Bishop Scarmuzzo, I would like to give you my confession," she whispered.

Antwan nearly fainted.

But before he could say a word, the widow began confessing her sins.

Lots of sins.

To Antwan, as a consummate ladies' man and a consistent sinner, they seemed like relatively innocuous transgressions... until she got to the part about having cheated on her husband throughout their marriage. In fact, she began to list names... and more names... and even more names.

Antwan stood there in shock. *Holy shit,* he thought. *She's more promiscuous than I am!*

The widow finally stopped and wiped away her tears, looking up at the Bishop. Antwan inhaled deeply, not knowing what to do. Finally, he stepped forward and made the sign of the cross over the woman's head, whispering, "I absolve you of your sins."

Then he hesitated. "And... um... please say twenty-five *Hail Marys* and... er... ten *Our Fathers*."

He paused again, his blue eyes sparkling with mischief this time.

"And please make a substantial donation to the Survivors Network of Those Abused by Catholic Priests."

He reached down and helped the redheaded widow up.

"Thank you so much, Bishop," she answered. "I have never confessed these transgressions to anyone. I'm so glad it was you and not someone local." The slightest hint of a leering smile creased her lovely face.

She took a step toward Antwan, gazing into his stunning eyes and touching him fondly on his arm. "I have most certainly heard of the Survivors Network. In fact, Richard was abused by a priest at a very young age."

She paused, and then revealed, "The experience put him off sex. We never even consummated out marriage because of his experiences with that damn priest."

She took a breath, then asked, "How much do you think I should contribute?"

Bishop Antwan Scarmuzzo shrugged. "It's up to you," he answered softly. *Ten thousand dollars would be very nice,* he thought.

The widow stepped back and gazed out the window, apparently lost in thought.

"How about one million dollars? For my sins?"

Antwan nearly fainted again.

"Ah... that would be most generous of you."

The widow sighed with relief.

She turned away from the window and took Antwan by the elbow to lead him out of the room. All the while, she was thinking, *Too bad he's a bishop. I've never seen such deep, gorgeous blue eyes before.*

At the bottom of the stairs, she opened the front door and nodded at Antwan. "I'll make the donation today as soon as you leave. I'll call the Network with my pledge and wire the money."

And her smile turned joyful.

●●●●●●●●●●●●●

Ruth Jackson lived up to her word and called the Network after the clergymen left her mansion. It was Saturday, but she still contacted her personal banker and brought him into the call. Once she explained to the young man on the other end what she wanted to accomplish, she was quickly put in touch with the president of the association, who was in the middle of a golf game with members of the Network's board of directors. Ruth listened impatiently as her banker and the president worked out wire transfers for one million dollars to go out immediately.

And it did.

The widow laughed to herself. Being worth over a billion dollars had its advantages!

•••••••••••••

Later, the widow was sipping her second flute of 1959 Dom Perignon champagne to celebrate her long-awaited confession and the donation to the Network. The bottle was worth over forty thousand dollars... and it tasted delicious.

She heard the doorbell ring. Since she was not expecting any more visitors, she let the butler answer it.

She sipped her bubbly and gazed out the window at the stunning autumn leaves. She loved this time of year. Her enormous lawn was filled with red oak and scarlet maple leaves. Some leaves were orange, and her favorite sycamore was a gorgeous, glowing yellow. She flashed back to when she was growing up in Minnesota, helping her father rake leaves and remembering the wonderful aroma of the burning leaf pile. She was sniffing the air as if she could smell the distinctive burning scent just as Albert appeared in the doorway with a panicked look on his face.

"Ma'am, Bishop Cousins and Father Taylor Fitzpatrick are here to see you."

The widow quickly stood up, spilling a bit of the expensive champagne on the front of her blouse. Bishop Cousins must have seen the elegant chalice and wanted to thank her for it.

"Well, show them in," she said as she refilled her glass to the brim, wondering if she had enough for her new guests and if she wanted to part with it.

Albert bowed slightly, as was his habit, and within a moment led the bishop and priest into the room. Father Taylor Fitzpatrick led the way with a holier-than-thou smile.

"Good evening, ma'am. It's so nice to finally meet you. I am Father Taylor Fitzpatrick."

And the lovely widow fainted.

••••••••••••

Antwan carefully unwrapped the chalice and set it down on Ted's kitchen table with reverence.

Ted's eyes nearly bulged out of his head. Gasping, he sank down into the nearest chair.

"Oh my God, that's... it's..."

"Beautiful!" Brian opined.

"Yes, beautiful," echoed Fritz, as he tore his white priest collar to shreds.

Ted opened his fridge and handed out cold bottles of beer, and a Diet Coke to Fritz.

Fritz grimaced and handed it back to him. "Not today, bro. Today, I'm having a beer with you. This is a celebration."

He stopped and considered his dear friends. "A goddamn celebration!" he repeated.

•••••••••••

Ruth Jackson sat up straight on her elegant couch after Albert broke open a capsule of smelling salts under her freckled nose. She looked around the room, not immediately recognizing where she was.

And then it all came rushing back to her.

She looked at this new Father Fitzpatrick, who was standing behind Albert with an impatient, sour expression. She glanced at Bishop Cousins, who was crouching next to the fireplace and smoking a cigarette. The fireplace was not lit and the flue was closed, but apparently that was lost on the Archbishop. He puffed like a smelly chimney and as if there was no tomorrow.

And from the way he consumed his cancer sticks, perhaps that was true.

Ruth stared at Father Fitzpatrick. "You're not Father Fitzpatrick!" she exclaimed.

The priest looked around with a confused expression. "Well, I actually am. Father Taylor Fitzpatrick of the Milwaukee diocese," he stated firmly.

Ruth swung her legs over the couch and shook her head. "No, he was just here this afternoon, and you don't look anything like him," she stated just as firmly.

The priest sucked in a frustrated breath and held his arms out at his sides—as if to say, *I don't know what to tell you.*

Albert handed the widow a refilled champagne glass and delicately interrupted. "Ma'am, if you don't mind, perhaps you would like me to explain?"

The lovely redhead nodded and took a hefty swallow of the alcohol, not even tasting it.

Albert methodically described what had happened in the afternoon meeting between another Father Fitzpatrick and Bishop Scarmuzzo. He further explained that Archbishop Cousins did not get out of the limousine, as he was ostensibly on a call with the Vatican—the pope, actually. Then he explained how the bishop had picked out the most valuable of Richard Jackson's chalices and taken it with him.

Now it was the Archbishop's turn to faint.

•••••••••••

As the friends drank their ice-cold beers and silently observed the chalice, it was Fritz who broke the stillness.

"Okay, guys, so now what? We have this stunning chalice, but I've got to tell you, just looking at it makes me nervous. I mean, this is not like shoplifting. Look at that beautiful piece. It looks damn near priceless."

Ted jumped in. "Fritz is right. This isn't a steak that you slide inside your jacket at the grocery store. This is going to attract lots of attention and the police. And the church will do everything to get it back."

Brian finished a swig of his beer. "I agree. And come to think of it, how would we get rid of it? A freaking fence?" He was starting to tremble. "I really have no idea. Hell, I've never stolen anything but this in my life."

It was Antwan's turn now. "I have an answer to 'now what,' but first I'd like to tell you about my time alone with Ruth Jackson and what she is going to be doing for our cause," he interjected.

When he had everyone's attention, he proceeded to explain that Richard Jackson had been abused by a Catholic priest in his youth and that Ruth, in light of that, was going to donate one million dollars to the Survivors Network.

Antwan deliberately left out the part about Ruth's peccadillos and Richard not being able to consummate their marriage.

While his friends were dumbfounded, Antwan continued. "So I propose that we simply return this. I know it doesn't accomplish our goal of making a few bucks for ourselves, but a million dollars for the Survivors Network is more than enough for me."

Brian and Ted nodded in agreement, but Fritz shook his head. "I'm not sure about that. What if she didn't call? After all, the real archbishop was there right after us. I'm guessing she scrapped the whole idea of a donation and is at the police station looking at mug shots."

"Damn it, he's right," moaned Ted.

Fritz took another sip of his beer and pointed the half-empty bottle at Ted.

"You know what? Maybe she followed through, and maybe she didn't." He took another sip. "So why don't we call the Network and ask?"

Brian typed something into his ever-present computer. "Here's the number," he said an instant later.

Ted held up a finger. "Wait a second."

He disappeared for a few minutes, quickly returning with an unused nonregistered cell phone. "Let's use this phone."

Fritz laughed out loud. "What the hell are you doing with that?"

Ted smirked. "I read too darn many crime novels, and the bad guys are always using throwaway cell phones, so I went out and bought one just to have it handy."

Antwan took the phone from him and saw that it was partially charged. Dialing the number, he put his finger to his lips for silence.

After a short runaround, Antwan was finally talking to the Network's president, Tim Helbit.

"Hey, Tim, this is Albert…"

He hesitated, and then pulled a last name out of the air.

"…Palmer, calling on behalf of Ruth Jackson."

Tim responded immediately. "Yes, Albert, how are you today? Thank you for following up. I can't tell you how happy we are with Mrs. Jackson's generous donation. All of us are walking on air here. The wire came through as expected, and we are most grateful. It is the largest donation we have ever had… by far!"

The man actually giggled.

"I mean, really, a million dollars! It's like manna from heaven!"

The phony Albert Palmer beamed jubilantly at his friends. "Well, that's wonderful. We just wanted to follow up to make sure that you received the funds."

"Oh, absolutely. They're in our savings account, and I must tell you that I keep going online and looking at it once every fifteen minutes to make sure I'm not dreaming."

He giggled again. "But Mr. Palmer, as long as I have you on the line, perhaps you could make a suggestion. I know

Wisconsin and Milwaukee have seen dozens of victims that we haven't had contact with. So, do you know a few worthy victims? All of us here at the Network would appreciate their names."

He paused. "It's a little too soon to know how much each victim will receive, but the Board of Directors are thinking about twenty-five thousand dollars for each victim... at least."

Now, Antwan was the one who wanted to giggle.

"Yes, absolutely. I have a few names in mind, all victims of Father Franklin Recker."

He hesitated. "But why don't I have each of them call you directly. After all, this would be between you and them, strictly confidential, I assume?"

"That would be wonderful, Albert. Franklin Recker was one of the worst. We would really appreciate the names."

The faux Albert agreed, and then added firmly, "By the way, Tim, you and I never had this conversation!"

Tim immediately responded, this time with a somber tone. "Absolutely. We take our fiduciary responsibilities very seriously here at the Network."

Then he chuckled quietly. "Albert Palmer... Who? Never heard of you!"

•••••••••••••

Albert had shown the clergymen out of the house as Ruth Jackson finished the expensive bottle of champagne.

The archbishop and the real Father Fitzpatrick had suggested that the police be called immediately.

But Ruth differed. She needed time to think this through.

As she sipped the last of her bubbly, she thought to herself that the first bishop and the bogus Father Fitzpatrick were actually nicer than the real ones.

By far!

The first set had been respectful and polite. The bishop from Boston had incredible, deep blue eyes that seemed to glisten with compassion and understanding.

She tried not to think impure thoughts.

On the other hand, the second set of clergymen were... well... pompous and holier-than-thou. She wrinkled her nose at the memory of the chain-smoking archbishop; she could still smell the nasty smoke on her clothing.

P.U.!

Also, the self-righteous Father Fitzpatrick had insisted on calling the police immediately.

That had stopped Ruth in her tracks. After all, the chalices were still technically hers. So Ruth deferred making a decision instantly and now was thinking about opening another bottle of the ungodly expensive Dom Perignon before heading up to bed.

She actually smiled as she thought about her confession to the false bishop.

Better him than the human chimney.

•••••••••••

It was midnight when the group, who had passed their time playing poker, piled into Ted's automobile.

Since Fritz was pretty much too drunk to drive, Ted was at the wheel. They headed across town to the widow's mansion, and Antwan held the repackaged chalice in his lap. He had surreptitiously inserted a brief note into an envelope inside the box before sealing it.

As the car pulled up to the curb next to the mansion's gates, Antwan passed the boxed-up chalice to Brian. He was the fastest runner of the group, and he would perhaps need to make a rapid getaway. Brian took the package and quickly got out of the automobile before it sped off and headed around the block.

Brian peeked around the brick pillar at the side of the gate and confirmed that the long driveway and the yard were unoccupied. They were only lit up by small in-ground lights. He trotted up to the front door and gingerly placed the boxed chalice on the stoop, then rang the doorbell twice. As he was about to leave, he spotted a doorknocker in the shape of a lion's head. For good measure, he rapped it loudly.

BAM BAM BAM!

Then he sprinted down the driveway.

The car was now idling at the curb with one of its passenger doors already open. Brian leapt in nimbly, slamming the door shut behind him with an unmistakable thud.

The poker players roared away with pious grins on their faces.

•••••••••••

Thinking that she'd heard the doorbell ring, Ruth Jackson rolled over and covered her head with a pillow. Then she heard the deafening clamor of the doorknocker, and she sat bolt upright in her bed.

She was still a bit tipsy.

Flinging her legs over the bedside, she pulled on her thick pink robe, slipped into her slippers, and headed down the stairs to the front door. She switched on the exterior lights and the stoop light as well. The yard and the lawn lit up as if it were high noon.

Peeking through the peephole, she saw nothing. Ruth started to open the door but stopped, wishing that Albert was a live-in butler. She had no idea who was out there.

So she turned away from the front door, making sure it was still bolted from the inside. Then she detoured through the house to Richard's den, where she had a view of the front door stoop.

Gently, she parted the curtains.

She sighed with relief.

No one was at the door, but she thought she saw a small package in the light. She looked at the old-fashioned phone on the desk and considered calling the police.

After all, she had no idea what was in the package. Perhaps a bomb?

So she picked up the ancient-looking receiver and began to dial the police.

A sleepy, gruff officer with a gravelly smoker's voice answered the phone. "Shorewood police, Sergeant Billows."

Ruth hesitated. "I'm sorry, I have the wrong number," she finally said.

She slammed down the old-fashioned receiver in its cradle, startling even herself.

Parting the curtain, she looked out the window. Sure enough, the box was still sitting there.

She stroked her chin, just as her husband used to do when he was contemplating something problematic. "What would Richard have done?" she asked herself.

The answer came immediately, as if Richard were standing next to her. *"Open the goddamn door and retrieve the package! This isn't the freaking airport,"* he would have said.

So that was what she did.

•••••••••••••

The poker players returned to Ted's place filled to the gills with adrenaline and opened another round of beers for good measure. Then they sat down at the poker table and resumed their game in silence. No one spoke for quite a while.

The men were all busy thinking about whether they would contact the Network and give up their names.

And of course Fritz was winning, but no one accused him of cheating this time.

Ted snipped the end off a King of Denmark cigar that he'd been saving for a special occasion. Once he got it started, he looked at his friends through the smoke and finally broke the silence.

"I don't know about you, but I'm calling the Network tomorrow and getting my name in the hat for some remuneration."

He pronounced each syllable: *re-mun-er-a-tion.*

He puffed on his cigar and blew a stinky smoke ring at the ceiling as he continued. "I don't care if it comes back to haunt me. What the hell did we do? Borrowed a chalice for a few hours. Who the hell cares! And besides," he added with a snide smirk, "the widow didn't even see me."

Antwan shook his head in amazement, then took a swallow from his latest Guinness Stout. "Oh, easy for you to say. I got right up in Ruth's face—and beard or no beard, she might recognize me."

All the while, he was thinking about Ruth's confession and how distraught she would be about confessing her sins to a counterfeit bishop.

Brian leaned forward with a beer in hand. "Yeah, I agree with Antwan, and I didn't have a beard to hide my face! Damn it, she could recognize me in a New York minute. I'm not sure it's worth twenty-five thousand dollars from the Network." He grimaced. "I don't think I would do well in prison."

Fritz chuckled half-heartedly. "Hell, my gay friend, you would be the life of the party."

He sipped his Diet Coke, looking longingly at Antwan's Guinness. "But none of you really needs to worry."

He put the can of Diet Coke on the table in front of him. "Here is what I'm thinking. Why don't we just hold off on calling the Network for a few days? If the lovely widow calls the police, it will certainly end up in the papers."

He looked down at his poker hand. "If she doesn't call the cops, then go ahead and call the Network and get your just rewards."

He spread out his cards in front of him with a shit-eating grin on his face. "Oh, by the way, I win."

The rest of the players tossed in their cards, grumbling good-naturedly.

"So what else is new?" Ted mumbled, looking across the table at Brian and shooting a smoke ring at him.

Antwan finished the last of his dark beer, belched, and then glanced at the clock on the wall. "Hey, do you know what day it is?"

Ted puffed on his cigar and shrugged. "Sure, November first. What of it?"

Antwan blew over the top of his empty beer bottle, filling the small room with an eerie, ghost-like sound.

"It's All Saints' Day," he said in a creepy staccato voice.

Grimacing, Antwan leaned forward and put the empty bottle on the card table. "So, do you guys feel like saints after returning that damn chalice?"

Ted blew one last smoke ring at the yellowed ceiling and whispered, "Yes, I do indeed."

•••••••••••

Ruth Jackson was sipping on the last of the bottle of Dom Perignon and staring at the cardboard box. She had shaken it just like a Christmas present and was delighted that it did not blow her to kingdom come.

She sipped the bubbly again. After all, the champagne was very tasty.

When the flute was empty, she finally slit open the top of the neatly wrapped box with a kitchen knife and tossed the knife onto the kitchen counter. Then she lifted out the contents of the box … to find nothing but a neat lump of bubble wrap.

She giggled and burped.

"Well, whoever sent this was nice and tidy."

Cutting the tape on the bubble wrap, she carefully opened it and unrolled the contents.

She gasped.

Her chalice, undamaged, was sitting in the bubble wrap, and it gleamed under the bright kitchen lights. She gently picked up the chalice by the stem and pushed the wrapping to the floor. Then she reverently placed the chalice in front of her on the table.

She shook her head in amazement.

Standing up, she went to the wine fridge and took out the last bottle of the expensive champagne, deftly opening it with a practiced flourish. She filled her champagne flute and sat down, leaving the open bottle on the table. It was then that she noticed the envelope still clinging to the bubble wrap on the floor. She bent down and picked it up, then gasped again.

It was addressed to her.

In precise handwriting, the matte envelope declared:

To the lovely Ruth Jackson.

She exhaled and laughed very, very, softly.

Slitting the envelope open with one of her long red fingernails instead of the kitchen knife, she read the note quickly.

Dear Mrs. Jackson,

*I hope you are reading this with your wonderful chalice
sitting in front of you.*

My name is Bishop Scarmuzzo.

Just kidding.

*My name is Antwan and I was delighted to meet you at
your beautiful home and to have the opportunity of view-
ing all of the crucifixes and chalices.*

*I certainly am not a bishop, nor a priest, nor a regular
member of any church.*

But I was in my youth—most definitely.

*Just like your late husband, I had a… how should I say it…
an episode with a pedophile priest here in Milwaukee. So,
along with some of my friends who also had the same experience, we drummed up a harebrained scheme to steal a
chalice from the Catholic Church.*

I guess that's not right. It was your chalice.

*So we thought we would steal it from you, and for that we
apologize most sincerely. Our little band of priest victims
justified it by thinking it would compensate us for the
heartache we have suffered over the years.*

In hindsight, that was a mistake on our part.

And all of us would like to apologize once again.

So now the chalice is hopefully back in your hands, no worse for the wear. Just think of it as having taken a little field trip.

Chalices need a little adventure, too.

Respectfully,

Non-Bishop Antwan

P.S. Your beautiful confession is held next to my heart, and just like a real priest or bishop, I will never tell anyone. That is my solemn promise to you.

•••••••••••••

Ruth read the note over and over again, then finally wiped away her tears. Pouring the contents of her champagne flute into the chalice, the widow raised it to her lips and took a sip. Gently putting the gorgeous chalice down in front of her, she laughed silently to herself and made a decision.

She was not going to give this chalice to the Catholic Church—or any other chalices, for that matter.

"Hell, it might come in handy for mimosas."

As she beheld the handsome vessel in front of her, she whispered, "God bless you, Antwan."

Then she paused and added, "And the many other victims."

She raised the chalice and held it out in front of her for a toast with a joyful, tearful smile on her face.

"God bless them all."

No Horsing Around

Ragnar Luther Hemlock was small. So small, in fact, he'd earned the highly ironic nickname of Hercules. A lifelong self-described "criminal of opportunity," he'd stolen his first car at the age of eleven and never looked back. Then when he turned sixteen, he graduated to sticking up Seven-Elevens and other convenience stores. At twenty-eight, he robbed his first bank. Then, at thirty-one, he discovered that most cities have illegal poker games played by wealthy high-rollers who don't call the police when relieved of their winnings.

It was exactly this crime that Hercules had recently committed in Minneapolis. But, since he'd learned to quickly disappear after a job, he was headed for Des Moines as fast as his Lincoln Town Car could carry him. He was slurping on a large Dairy Queen vanilla cone, trying not to slop it on his natty clothes. But it was the Fourth of July and hotter than a pistol, so he was having little success.

As Hercules licked the melting ice cream, he laughed to himself about his latest caper. He'd taken a seat in a high-stakes game in a private suite at the new Intercontinental at the airport. Per usual, he played the first round, not really caring about the outcome. He was more interested in observing—figuring out who was carrying, seeing who was getting drunk and, God forbid, who was doing both—a potentially powerful combination.

In this instance, none of the other players had a handgun, but Hercules quickly figured out that one of the guys, an enormous Austrian, had clearly been in the country's special ops, since he was carrying one of the most deadly knives ever designed. It was a seven-inch pewter-colored killer with a glass breaker on the tip of the handle. Hercules took the knife, just in case he ever needed to break some glass, along with every nickel in the room. Just for good measure, he duct-taped the other players' mouths, hands, and feet before getting the hell out of there.

As Hercules finished his cone, he looked down and sighed. He'd dripped ice cream on his favorite leather pants, so he slowed down abruptly, grabbed a napkin from the glove box, and damn near got rear-ended when the driver behind him slammed on the brakes. As the rusty, ancient truck swerved around the Lincoln, the driver gave him the finger.

And Hercules caught his breath.

The finger belonged to the most beautiful woman he'd ever seen. She had long, raven-black hair, glowing olive skin, and a perfect nose, which was flanked by a pair of impossibly high cheekbones. Even though she was frowning, Hercules could see that her almond-shaped eyes were the color of cat's eye stones as she roared off into the shimmering heat, leaving him in a cloud of Iowa dust.

But not for long.

Hercules threw the soiled napkin on the floor, stomped on the accelerator, and sped off after her without thinking twice.

Mary Teresa Arrowood, the driver, was a kindergarten teacher and, as her last name implied, straight as an arrow. She was headed to her parents' farm on the outskirts of Des Moines, and she was looking forward to riding Ace, her Arabian, and watching the fireworks.

Mary Teresa didn't notice the Lincoln following her. She passed the small airport where the annual fireworks show took place after dark. A quarter mile later, she pulled into the farm, where a large For Sale sign stood in the front yard, and parked next to the barn. Reminding herself to remember to feed the hogs, she scooted into the barn and hurried to Ace's stall with an apple in her hand.

The gorgeous horse loved apples almost as much as sugar cubes, so he greeted her with an affectionate nudge and made quick work of the fruit. Mary Teresa gave him a hug, then saddled him and headed down the highway, totally forgetting about the hogs. Both sides of the highway were starting to fill up with cars. As Mary Teresa and Ace trotted along, they could see people carrying lawn chairs, blankets, coolers full of beer, and cans of bug spray.

Given the heat, Mary Teresa decided to make the ride short. Besides, she'd forgotten to feed the hogs. As Ace carried her down the road, she thought about the past few months. Her father, George, had died in January, and her mother, Grace, was still in shock, since he'd only left a small life insurance policy—just enough to bury him and cover nearly a year's worth of mortgage payments.

Hence the for-sale sign.

Mary Teresa tugged gently on Ace's reins, turning him back toward the farm. Her mother was visiting her brother in Chicago, so Mary Teresa had the house to herself for the holiday weekend. She was looking forward to watching the fireworks from the screened-in porch with a glass of wine and no mosquitos. She turned into the gravel driveway and rode up to the barn. Right behind her truck, blocking her in, was a new Lincoln Town Car. *Gosh darn,* she thought to herself, *how rude!*

As Ace led her into the barn, she spotted a man standing by the far door that led to the hog pens. He was the ugliest man Mary Teresa had ever seen, yet he was dressed very well, albeit inappropriately for the heat. He was wearing leather pants, a long-sleeved shirt, and expensive alligator slip-ons. As he strode toward her, Ace immediately shied away, setting off alarm bells in Mary Teresa's mind. Ace had a sixth sense about humans, and he could always tell good from evil.

She quickly dismounted Ace and led him to his stall. The ugly man followed her. "Saw the for-sale sign in your yard," he said, smiling coolly. "I've always wanted a hobby farm, and I've just come into quite a bit of money, so I thought I'd take a look. Little did I know I'd find the most beautiful creature God has ever created."

Mary Teresa frowned and stepped back. "I'm sorry, but you'll need to make an appointment to see the place, so please call us after the holiday," she said politely, nodding toward the open door. "And now if you'll excuse me, I need to feed the hogs before the fireworks start," she said, walking down the barn aisle to fetch the wheelbarrow.   "Not so fast," he leered, stepping closer. "What's your name?"

She hesitated. "Mary Teresa. What's yours?"

He gave her an evil smile. "Ragnar Luther Hemlock, but they call me Hercules."

Mary Teresa started laughing. She tried to stop herself, but she couldn't. She laughed and laughed until snot was streaming out of her nose.

Hercules was not amused. Rage enveloped him and he saw his own fireworks behind his dark eyes. He pulled his new knife out from behind his back and shook it in Mary Teresa's face. She choked and spun around, then ran toward Ace's stall, where he was anxiously pawing the ground.

Hercules gave chase, still wielding the knife in front of him, when the horse bolted toward the intruder. Hercules stopped, dropped his knife, and looked around for a way to escape the charging horse. He ran out of the barn toward the hog pens with Ace right behind him, snorting and neighing. Hercules could feel the horse's hot breath on his neck when the Arabian shot past him and stopped short.

The horse reared up on his hind legs and kicked his front hooves like a prize fighter, nearly decapitating Hercules.

The man ducked and sprinted toward a solid four-foot fence in front of the hog pens. He hiked up his leather pants and clambered over it with Ace right behind him. With a push from Ace's long nose, Hercules landed on the other side of the fence in a pile of hog shit. Slipping and sliding in his alligator loafers, Hercules did his best to stand up, coming face to face with the largest hog he'd ever seen. As he stared into the massive animal's eyes, he could have sworn it was grinning at him. Hercules took a step backward, flattened himself against the fence, and tried to climb out of the pen.

No luck.

The hog, who Mary Teresa had christened Tiny, grabbed Hercules by the back of his pants. Tiny turned in a slow circle, headed for the corner of the pen, and began to chow down on Hercules while the other hogs waited patiently for any leftovers.

Mary Teresa, who had witnessed Ace's heroics, raced toward the hog pen. She hugged the horse and fed him a handful of sugar cubes. He stood steady while she hoisted herself onto his back. As she looked into the hog pen, she gasped. Tiny was crunching on Hercules' bloody head and groaning with delight. She stifled the urge to vomit, tugging on Ace's reins to guide the horse toward the highway. The fireworks were starting, so she urged Ace toward the airport so they could watch the show.

When the fireworks were nearly over, Mary Teresa and Ace made their way back to the farm. To her surprise, Hercules' shiny Lincoln was still running. She hopped off Ace's back and tied his reins to the fence. She opened the door, slid behind the wheel, and moved the car next to her truck. She pulled the keys out of the ignition and, on a hunch, pressed the button to open the trunk.

Mary Teresa walked around the car and gasped. The trunk was filled with stacks and stacks of crisp $100 bills. Ace snorted as Mary Teresa ran her hands over the money, then hugged herself and giggled. As the last fireworks illuminated the night sky, she ran over to the for-sale sign, pulled it out of the ground, and threw it aside. Ace whinnied happily.

"Ace, you are one hundred percent right," she laughed. "The farm is ours forever!"

Abruptly Heaven

William Beaker, age 27, was having the worst year of his life.

He'd lost his father to a heart attack, the rest of his family in a car crash, and Jake, his golden retriever, to causes unknown. Then, today—Christmas Eve—his fiancée dumped him. It was a snowy day and William (never Bill) was truly alone. He was so depressed he was thinking of offing himself.

William's father, William Beaker, Sr., had been diagnosed with brain cancer in late March. He was doing fairly well in spite of a nasty chemotherapy routine at the Mayo Clinic. In late June, William was driving his mother and younger brother and sister to the clinic for a visit when a drunk driver crossed the median on Highway 52 and killed everyone.

Except William.

His mother, who never wore a seatbelt, was killed instantly. The twins, who were in the back seat, took the brunt of the collision and were pronounced dead at the Mayo emergency room. William's father clutched his chest when he heard about the crash. Within moments of hearing the news, he suffered a massive heart attack and died.

Thanks to his airbag, William survived but had to spend six months with casts on both forearms. He didn't eat well, if at all. He lost quite a bit of weight, which didn't suit his tall, thin frame. Gaunt and depressed, William found himself on the Internet, searching for an innocuous but effective way of leaving this world behind.

He sighed woefully, not finding a suitable method. Too depressed to search any further, he was about to shut down his computer when he noticed the photo icon on his desktop. He clicked on the icon and there they were.

His family.

All smiles.

In a photo from last December, they were all playing in the snow at the Iverson Park ski jump. In another photo, William was soaring off the snow-packed slope into the blue sunny sky, a look of utter joy on his face.

At that moment, he roused himself. He got up from his chair and looked out the window at the snow-covered yard. He nodded to himself. Maybe, just maybe, he could jump to his death. Hell, he had damn near killed himself more times than he could count on the Iverson Park jump.

What the hell, William thought to himself. *It's worth a try.*

He turned off the computer and put on his winter gear. He headed to the garage and pulled out his jumping skis, aptly named D3 Nightmare Jumpers, and began walking through the blowing snow to the park.

Iverson Park was less than four blocks from William's house. By the time he arrived, it was dusk and there was no one in sight. He pulled his stocking cap down around his ears, balanced the skis on his right shoulder, and climbed up the steep stairs.

When he reached the top, he could see that the snow was well-packed, a sign that the jump had been recently used. He strapped the Nightmares to his feet and stood for a moment, feeling the strong wind gusts. He made the sign of the cross and pushed off for the last jump of his life.

Or so he thought.

As his skis picked up speed, William was astounded by the velocity of the wind. He had been jumping at Iverson Park since he was in grade school and had never experienced this kind of wind before. As he flew off the end of the jump, he leaned forward and pushed his ski tips down. His frozen nose was nearly touching the ends of his skis when another, even stronger gust of wind caught him and pushed him upwards.

And up.

And up.

William felt a moment of panic as, instead of falling down towards the snow, he was being pushed in the opposite direction, up towards the dark gray winter sky. As his ski tips pierced the thick layer of low-hanging clouds, he saw another layer of clouds, only this time they were blue. At that moment, he tried to take a deep breath but there was no oxygen. He hastily made the sign of the cross one more time and passed out.

The next thing he knew, he was warm.

From within.

He felt a golden radiance move through his body, from the top of his head down to his toes. As he burst through another layer of clouds, William tried to take another breath. When he felt a hand beneath each of his elbows, he looked to his right and then to his left.

To his astonishment, two beautiful angels were lifting him up.

And up.

And up.

William trembled as the trio burst through the ozone layer and headed towards outer space. They kept going for what seemed like an eternity until, in front of them, there was a silver cloud. In the middle of the cloud was a colossal gate encrusted with glowing pearls.

Saint Peter was standing next to the gate, wearing a mischievous grin on his weathered face and holding a large key in his hand. The angels set William down gently next to the saint. They kissed him tenderly on the cheek and disappeared. Saint Peter stepped in front of the gate, then unlocked it and motioned to William.

William looked down, realizing that his skis were no longer attached to his feet. He moved tentatively through the gate. Less than forty feet away, his family was clustered around the Lord Jesus Christ, who was seated on a golden throne with a divine smile on his face. At his feet was Jake, William's beloved golden retriever.

Christ whispered to Jake and the dog sprinted over to William, wagging his tail. He jumped up and put his front paws on William's chest and joyfully licked his face.

William giggled as he looked over the dog's shoulder at his family. Christ winked at William. "Welcome home," he said with a smile. "And Merry Christmas."

Sherlock and Tiger

Teresa Garcia Asia Ramirez, a dual citizen of the U.S. and Mexico and currently a rookie Los Angeles detective grade one, was pregnant.

Extremely pregnant.

She should have been on maternity leave, but she was a stubborn soul, and her partner would have been lost without her. Los Angeles detective grade three Samuel Watson, nicknamed Sherlock, was old enough to be Teresa's grandfather. The man had recently lost his wife to cancer, and it had soured him on life. Her name was Roxanne, Rox for short, and she did not take to chemotherapy at all. It was a painful process for her, and even more painful for Sherlock, who suffered right alongside the love of his life until, moaning from the pain, she passed away in the hospital. Afterward, Sherlock started to kill himself with alcohol and daytime soap operas.

At least that's what Sherlock joked about—the soaps, not the booze.

So, Teresa interceded, and Sherlock was back on the job, sober at least until five o'clock. She had gotten an early morning call from him and was headed to the cliffs overlooking Hollywood, where the very wealthy, including the film stars and producers, looked down at the homeless and peons in the slums below.

Nicknamed Holly-weird.

She pulled up to the Rockefeller mansion, a miniature Buckingham Palace, and as she exited her car, she noted that her partner was chatting with a couple of Hollywood's finest, taking notes and nodding. With some effort, Teresa pulled herself out of her nondescript, ancient, unmarked police car and waddled up to the police officers and Sherlock. The officers were young, crisp, and full of themselves but greeted Teresa affectionately. They knew what she was doing for her partner. Sherlock was a legend not only in the Hollywood precinct but throughout all of Los Angeles. In his prime, he had the best clearance record of any detective in the entire metro area. Additionally, he had turned down a more lucrative position in the Los Angeles police department to stay with his lowly Hollywood precinct. He liked to joke that the homeless would be lost without him, and perhaps they would. Sherlock donated a substantial portion of his net worth to those without a roof over their heads and to the homeless shelters that took care of them. On the weekends, he even cooked in Saint Mary's shelter and was famous for his spicy spaghetti and Italian bread.

The officers greeted Teresa by her nickname, Tiger, a bastardization of her initials, TGAR.

The youngest officer, Tad Bailey, a muscle-bound man of limited stature, gestured at her rotund belly.

"Hey Tiger, you have got to lay off the beer; you have quite the beer belly going!" he exclaimed. He had an obnoxiously squeaky voice that reminded Teresa of fingernails on a chalkboard. And of course, his nickname was indeed Squeaky.

The Holly-weird precinct apparently was big on nicknames.

Sherlock bellowed out a deep staccato laugh with a twinkle in his luminescent green eyes.

"Hey there, Squeaky, you have got to lay off the steroids; maybe substitute a beer now and then?"

Officer Bailey, in his tailored short-sleeved shirt, flexed and grinned at Sherlock, knowing damn well that the officers were tested on a regular basis for drugs and that steroids were not tolerated.

Just then, the matron of the house opened the front door and stepped out into the sunshine and humidity. Ruth Rockefeller, with a cascade of stunning golden blonde hair and a body like a twenty-five-year-old, her large chest preceding her out the door, nodded at the detectives with a quizzical look on her face.

"Well, what are you waiting for? The crime has been committed in here, not out in the sunshine."

Sherlock winked at Teresa and moved up the front steps nimbly, while Teresa, as big as a whale, not so much. The woman stood just inside the door waiting impatiently, and Sherlock flipped out his detective's badge and shook hands with Ruth. Teresa did the same, smiling her best cop smile at the woman who up close was not as old as she had surmised. Her face was tan and smooth, with no wrinkles in sight.

"I'm sorry, ma'am, my partner was waiting for me; as you can see, I don't move so well these days."

The woman scowled, turned, and led the way up the stairs, tossing a snide comment over her shoulder. "I'm afraid that means nothing to me; I don't care for children, especially nonwhite children."

Teresa shook her head as she waddled after the racist citizen. She glanced over at Sherlock as he pointed his finger at the woman's back, mimicking shooting her, and winked at Teresa.

Teresa simply bit her tongue.

Ruth led them into a large, immaculate study with not a trace of dust anywhere and Brazilian hardwood floors so shiny that one could almost see a reflection in them. The young matron of the house led them to a safe that stood open and empty, then turned toward the detectives and pointed.

"I have been robbed, and at the worst possible moment." And her scowl reappeared.

Sherlock peered inside the thick safe, then looked on the other side of it, noting that it was an old-fashioned combination lock unit.

"So, what was in the safe, ma'am?"

Ruth took out a printed list of items with photos of the safe's contents attached. Sherlock glanced at it and handed it to Teresa, who noted that one of the last entries had been crossed off. She squinted her baby-blue eyes and said out loud, "Ten stamp collections, EXTREMELY valuable."

Ruth let out an unladylike grunt.

"Yes, they were the most valuable things in the safe, worth more than one million dollars."

She paused, and her scowl was replaced with a half-smile.

"Thank God the collection was out being appraised or my husband the idiot would have been devastated; he actually owns the collection."

Teresa nodded. "Can I keep this list, ma'am?"

Ruth returned the nod. "Of course, that's why I printed it, and stop calling me ma'am."

Teresa began to roll her eyes back into her head but caught herself just in time. "Yes, Mrs. Rockefeller."

Ruth's scowl returned. "Oh please, not Mrs. How about Miss., since I am about to get divorced."

Sherlock stepped forward. "Well, that is interesting, ma'am... I mean, Ms. Tell me about that."

"Why? What does that have to do with anything?"

Sherlock pursed his lips in disdain. "Well, perhaps your soon-to-be-divorced husband thought to relieve you of the contents of the safe."

Ruth laughed a harsh cougher's woofing laugh. "Not a chance. My soon-to-be-ex has no idea that I'm planning on divorcing him."

And she laughed again.

"Hell, he would actually have to come home once in a while and give up the poker tables and the whores in Las Vegas."

Sherlock grimaced.

"So, if we checked on...." He paused and looked at his notes. "Davidson Rockefeller, he would say that he was in Vegas last night?"

Ruth snorted. "I would certainly think so, and please understand that I'm not sure when this... um... burglary happened. I have been with my soulmate, Mary Sweeney, at her home in Palm Springs for the last week. It wasn't until Maria called about the break-in that I hurried back. To be honest, the house really isn't used much anymore."

Teresa took a few notes and inhaled.

"So, let me get this straight—you are going to divorce Davidson, who spends his time in Las Vegas, and you were with Mary Sweeney?"

Ruth's scowl returned. "Well, that's what I just said; did I stutter? And by the way, my husband is actually named

David, not Davidson. He tells people that he is related to the New York Rockefellers, and one of the sons is named Davidson. He claims to be a close cousin and immensely wealthy."

Ruth snorted once again.

"The man doesn't have a pot to piss in, and half this house and everything in the safe belonged to me when the robbery occurred. I have been supporting him for over fifteen years simply because my parents required me to get married to get access to my trust."

Teresa wrote more notes. Ruth glared at Teresa's swollen belly.

"You see, I am gay, but my parents, who were born-again Christians, just wouldn't recognize it. So, I married David; he was my beard for fifteen agonizing years. But now that my parents have passed, I am free to do what I please. And that is to get married to Mary and the hell with David!"

She hesitated.

"Things are different now. Nobody gives a rat's ass about whether you are a lesbian, a gay man, or a freakin' transvestite."

And she paused once more. "Except my freakin' parents, God rest their ornery souls."

Then she looked at her watch and turned.

"It's noon, and I need a drink. Come on down to the kitchen. I think I'll start my day with a Bloody Mary, since we are talking about my sweetheart, Mary Sweeney!"

And she was gone.

Sherlock sighed to himself and followed her down the stairs, but Teresa paused, looking around the immaculate den. She had never seen a room so clean—the paint had no dings in it at all, and there was no dust in sight; even the extra-small pieces on the tall armoire were dust-free.

She furrowed her brow. Unless Maria, the maid, or another cleaning person was over seven feet tall, Teresa wondered how they could clean that high without a ladder. A dust mop would simply knock the knick-knacks over, and they looked to be expensive.

She glanced up at the ceiling and saw a brand-new smoke alarm in the corner. Being the detective that she was, she could see it was new, since the center of the room had a faded yellow circle where the old smoke alarm had been. Somehow, Teresa felt better that at least something was not spotless and needed a fresh coat of paint. Something left her uneasy, though, and she just didn't know what it was. She shrugged and followed Sherlock down the stairs, or rather, waddled down the stairs, taking her time as she followed Sherlock's bellowing voice.

"No ma'am, it is a bit too early for me, and I really don't drink much these days anyway," Teresa heard as she entered the spacious kitchen. Maria was setting a huge

Bloody Mary in front of Ruth before she seemingly disappeared without leaving the room.

Ruth laughed softly at Sherlock's comment.

"Oh, don't bullshit me, detective; I can spot a fellow boozer when I see one," she said, leaning forward to sniff the detective. She smiled a real smile for the first time. "And I'm guessing you are a bourbon man, maybe a Maker's Mark drinker."

It was Sherlock's turn to smile.

"Only on special occasions, and I'm a Jack Daniels man, but not until after five o'clock."

Ruth nodded, took a sip of the Bloody Mary, and tilted her glass toward Sherlock. "Breakfast of champions!"

Maria appeared out of nowhere, set a cup of steaming black coffee in front of the detective, and disappeared back into the woodwork. Teresa sat uninvited on a kitchen counter stool that was too tall for her, but since she wanted to keep her distance from Ruth, who was sitting at the kitchen table, and observe her from a distance, she let her senior and more experienced partner ask the questions.

And he did, as he sipped the hot coffee.

"Now, Ms. Rockefeller, how many people have the combination to the safe?"

Ruth shook her head.

"No one, not even my soon-to-be-ex. The only person that has it besides me is my attorney."

Sherlock grimaced. "Really? Most combinations are fairly long. Are you sure you didn't write it down where he might have stumbled across it?"

She took a sip of the crimson cocktail and shivered with satisfaction as she tipped her head.

"No, detective; in spite of being a lush, I have a photographic memory. Passwords, checking account numbers, and credit card numbers are all right here. A simple safe combination is child's play."

And she smiled a catty smile.

"Hell, I even memorized the list I gave you of the safe contents, and I can recall every stamp in the collection. I picture them in my mind, and it's as if they were right in front of me. And I'll say it again, I am so glad that the collection was not in the safe. It was just a coincidence that it is being appraised, and lucky for me, because it was not insured."

And her scowl replaced her grin.

Again, Maria appeared as if by magic, this time setting a cold glass of orange juice in front of Teresa. Maria pursed her lips and nodded at Teresa's swollen belly, squinting her eyes at the mention of the stamp collection and its appraisal.

Teresa winked at her as Sherlock began to ask Ruth his good old routine questions.

"Who has a key to the house?" Answer: Ruth, her husband, and Maria.

"How many servants or helpers do you have?" Answer: Maria, along with occasional help from her granddaughter.

"Where is David Rockefeller staying in Las Vegas?" Answer: The Bellagio.

Et cetera.

Et cetera.

Et cetera.

And Teresa diligently took notes.

Ruth was on her second morning cocktail when Sherlock drained the last sip of coffee and stood up.

"We need to look into a few things, and we will be in touch. I would like to speak with your husband at the very least."

He motioned to Teresa, and she shadowed him through the door and out to her car.

"Well, Tiger, what do you think?"

Teresa looked up at the mini-mansion, catching a glimpse of Maria peeking out the window.

"I'm not sure, but I have a few guesses. One: that David, or Davidson, found out about the pending divorce and took the safe contents himself. Two: that she stole them herself. Three: she is lying, and they are not getting divorced, and they took them together. Four: there was a break-in, and somehow, she gave the combination to someone and was unaware of it."

She paused. "But I'm betting on good old Davidson."

Sherlock nodded. "Yeah, me too, and he is first on my list to check out. I know that Ms. Rockefeller is well-connected, but after all, this is a burglary and not a homicide."

•••••••••••••

Teresa was sitting on her tiny three-season porch sipping herbal tea and waiting for her fiancé to bring home Chinese takeout. It was past dusk, and the moon was shining a bright carroty color. Teresa watched as a cloud shaped like the head of a Tyrannosaurus rex prepared to swallow the carroty moon for supper.

And the pregnant detective's phone rang.

Sherlock's gravelly voice bellowed out of her cell.

"Hey Tiger, sorry about the late call, but I was wrong this afternoon."

"Really? About what?" asked Teresa as the wind blew the dinosaur cloud away, leaving the moon in all its glory.

"Well, I was wrong on both accounts regarding good old Mr. Davidson Rockefeller. First of all, he didn't steal anything, and second of all, we do have a homicide."

He paused.

"The gentleman in question was just found in the trunk of his car right behind the Hollywood sign on the hill, with quite a few holes in his chest and a very permanent frown on his face."

•••••••••••

Teresa pulled up to the winding, dusty road that led to the Hollywood sign and rolled down her window as a Hollywood cop she didn't recognize leaned down. She held out her detective's shield.

"Looking for Sam Watson," she said bluntly, her stomach growling.

The officer, a clean-cut African-American man wearing uniform pants with a starched crease that looked like you could cut yourself with it, looked at the shield and Teresa's ever-expanding belly and smiled a weary cop's smile.

"Yes ma'am, Sherlock's up there with the medical examiner and the officer that discovered the body."

And he hesitated.

"I've been told not to let any more cars up there, but looking at you, I'm sure not making you walk a quarter mile. So the hell with them."

And he hesitated again. "When are you due?"

Teresa patted her belly lovingly.

"Any moment now, and thanks. I would hate to give birth under the Hollywood sign. I wouldn't know what to name the kid."

The officer grinned. "Well, if it was a girl, you could call her Holly, and if it was a boy, you could call him Woody. Maybe Weird, for a middle name," he said, woofing a quiet laugh as he backed away from Teresa's car and waved her through.

As her car approached, Sherlock directed her to the area where his car was parked and sauntered over. Teresa was struggling to exit her car when Sherlock reached in and gently pulled her out, getting her to her feet with a grimace on his wrinkled old face.

"Son of a gun, I should've told you not to come up here. You need to be in bed watching late-night television and eating anchovy pizza."

Teresa sniffed and caught a whiff of whiskey.

"Yeah, right, and leave you alone to drink yourself to death. Not a chance. Besides, I hate anchovies."

Just then, the medical examiner, Rip Thorsten, a tall, thin, elderly man with a shaved head and a nose like a hawk, strode up, removing his protective gloves and lighting up a cigarette. Teresa scowled and did not comment, but the medical examiner waived his smoke away when he realized Teresa was pregnant. He held the cancer stick behind him and gestured toward the car.

"Sorry about that, Tiger, but after looking at my one-billionth gunshot wound, I need a smoke. In fact, a stiff drink would be just dandy. Whoever did this was either high as a kite or passionate about the victim."

Or both.

He turned and took a long puff on his cigarette and blew it into the wind. "The man was shot right in the trunk, and I haven't seen so much blood since Vietnam. Jesus, the man was swimming in it." He shook his head and spat.

"I'm getting too old for this shit," he added, looking at Teresa and her swollen belly. "And you, for Christ's sake—you're as big as a whale. What the hell are you doing here?"

Teresa rolled her eyes. "Yeah, yeah, I know—I should be home eating anchovy pizza," she said as her stomach growled loudly.

Rip took one more puff on his cigarette and ground it into the turf. "Well, it sure sounds like you need to eat something."

He stopped and turned toward the car. "I'll know more when I get him back to the lab, but he had a wallet with him and a driver's license. His name was David J. Rockefeller, and he wanted to have his organs donated."

And the medical examiner chuckled gruesomely. "Not going to happen now; after the autopsy, there won't be much left, unless someone wants that handsome nose," he remarked, stroking his own beak. "I'm guessing he was killed between eighteen and thirty-six hours ago, but I'll pin it down for you."

He waived at the car and nodded to the detectives. "But he is all yours for now," he said, patting Teresa on the shoulder. "Haven't you heard of maternity leave, Tiger? For Christ sakes, this is fucking California. I think you get to take a decade off."

He pulled out another cigarette and coughed a hacking smoker's cough. "And by the way, I like anchovy pizza."

•••••••••••••

The detectives bid a smoky goodbye to the medical examiner and made their way over to Davidson's car. For a man who didn't have a pot to pee in, it was quite the automobile: a late model, champagne-colored Bentley Mulsanne, with a list price between $250,000 and $300,000.

Unfortunately, Davidson was never going to drive it again, barring reincarnation.

Teresa looked over the trunk and pursed her lips, trying not to gag. The man had indeed been shot in the trunk, and he was awash in crimson blood and did indeed have a frown on his face... or more like a grimace.

Sherlock motioned toward the face, which was untouched.

"Ninety-nine percent of murders are done by a spouse, and even before I got here, I had figured it was our Bloody-Mary-drinking Ms. Ruth that did this. Especially with the divorce pending, but now I'm not so sure."

Teresa looked at him, perplexed. Sherlock pointed to the unscathed face and then to the bullet-riddled torso.

"Most women would shoot once or twice and would usually end with the face." And he paused. "Hell, maybe I'm wrong, but this sure does not look like the work of our morning drinker. Hell, she would have needed to stop in the middle of this carnage just to have a cocktail."

And he chuckled, mostly to himself. "I'm guessing whoever did this was high, probably on crystal meth or maybe cocaine. If you have ever watched a meth freak, their eyes are a giveaway." Sherlock looked at Teresa and flipped his own eyes back and forth. He then did it again and pointed his fist, now emulating a handgun, at Davidson's corpse, moving his hand back and forth with his eyes keeping pace. Teresa shrugged, not entirely convinced.

"If it was me, or Ruth, I would stay away from that handsome face. My God, Ms. Ruthie didn't say how good-looking the man was. He certainly belonged in Hollywood."

Sherlock grinned ruefully, bent down to sniff the body, and mimicked holding his nose.

"P.U., I guess he overdid it with his cologne."

And he winked at Teresa. "You are right; he belonged in Tinsel Town—handsome as hell, gay, and using the latest cologne. It's called Attract Men."

Teresa furrowed her brow. "You're just pulling my leg."

Sherlock laughed. "Not at all; just ask Squeaky."

And he laughed again. "He is gayer than a daffodil."

•••••••••••••

The next morning, Teresa had slept in and gotten to the station midmorning. Sherlock was talking on the phone to the manager of the Bellagio in Las Vegas. He put it on speaker, and Teresa plopped down in her desk chair and rolled over to listen in.

"I am so sorry to hear about Mr. Rockefeller; that is absolutely tragic. Has anyone let Peter know?"

Sherlock squinted and frowned. "Who is Peter?"

"Peter O'Brien, Mr. Rockefeller's... um... his... um... friend."

"Are you saying this Peter O'Brien is more than a friend?"

"Um... well... Mr. Rockefeller had many friends here in Vegas. He was very successful at what he did."

Sherlock gave Teresa a dubious glance, and she shrugged her shoulders and patted her tummy absentmindedly.

"Really? I did not know that. I was led to believe that he was... how shall I say it, and I quote someone that should know him well... that he didn't have a pot to pee in?"

The manager chortled. "Well, that's just not true." He paused. "Well, it was maybe ten years ago, but certainly not now. When Davidson first came to town, he was no gambler, but he decided to try everything. And he was pretty much awful at everything. Slots, blackjack, roulette, faro, sports betting… and he was abysmal at craps. So much so, that we would not let him play anymore. I mean, he lost with every throw of the dice. If the lousiest craps player was in Wikipedia, Mr. Rockefeller's picture would have been featured."

"Well, I'm sorry to hear that, though I don't gamble, and I never will, but you said he was successful now? What did he do? Park cars? Stand-up comic? Male model?"

The manager chortled again. "Well, he was unquestionably handsome enough to be a model, but no, he found his calling playing poker. It was as if he had been born for it, a gift from God. As God-awful as he was at craps, he set the world on fire at the poker table. And he could play every kind of poker, from stud poker to five-card draw to three-card brag. Heck, he even beat our Chinese guests at open-faced Chinese, and it drove them crazy.

"But his favorite game was Texas Hold 'Em. He loved to play, and he was one of the top five players in the world. Phil Hellmuth said if Davidson was on a roll, he couldn't be beat. And he was on a roll often, much to the Bellagio's chagrin. But he brought in outsiders that had never played or stayed at our hotel, so we welcomed him with open arms. In fact, he had a comped room that was his all year round—no charge, including meals and drinks."

The manager paused.

"I guess we can suspend that now that he is gone. What a shame, what a shame."

Teresa mouthed, "Peter O'Brien," and Sherlock nodded.

"I appreciate the information. I guess we were misinformed, but we would really like to speak with Mr. Peter O'Brien. Would you happen to have a phone number for him?"

"Sure, hold on for a moment."

Sherlock held his hand over the phone's receiver, shaking his head.

"I'm starting to wonder about our Bloody-Mary-sucking Ms. Ruth Rockefeller."

And he removed his hand from the speaker.

"Okay, 702-909-0221," he recited to Teresa, who diligently wrote it on her notepad. "Thank you for your help, sir. We will be in touch if anything else comes up." Sherlock nodded and replied, "Goodbye."

And disconnected.

Sherlock placed the old-fashioned receiver back in its cradle ever so gently. He sighed, pursed his lips, and looked Teresa directly in the eyes.

"Well, well, well, this is definitely getting interesting. People have a habit of lying to police just for the hell of it. But Ms. Ruthie, I think, is not what she appears."

And he picked up the phone and dialed Peter O'Brien, one of many friends of the deceased Davidson Rockefeller.

The phone was answered immediately with a quiet voice that seemed to be whispering to someone else.

"I'm sorry, I should have turned my phone off. Yes sir, that was my bad. I know you are paying for this lesson. I will just be a second."

And Peter, hopefully, whispered into the phone.

"Is it true—is David dead?"

Sherlock tilted his head.

"Um... hello... is this Mr. Peter O'Brien?"

"Well, heck yes, and who is this? I saw the LA area code, and I just had to answer."

"This is Detective Samuel Watson of the Hollywood division, and I am sorry to tell you your friend is deceased."

There was a long pause, and Sherlock heard an unfriendly conversation in the background.

A strained whisper came back on the line.

"My God, that is awful. I will be done with this lesson in thirty minutes, and I'll call you back. I see your number on my phone. This is just awful; my God... we were going to be married."

•••••••••••••

A humorous chuckle and a wry smirk emanated from Sherlock.

"Well, the plot thickens; Teresa, the plot certainly thickens. He was about to get married to Davidson Rockefeller. I'm guessing we can scratch Mr. Peter off our list of suspects."

And he smirked. "Or add him to it."

Teresa patted her tummy and shrugged.

"Never say never, but that didn't sound like a man that had killed someone. But maybe he has an alibi, and maybe he doesn't. If you say Ms. Rockefeller didn't do it—and by the way, I'm not convinced of that—then someone needed to. Las Vegas is just close enough to Los Angeles to give any-one overnight access and a quick trip back to Sin City."

Sherlock smiled benevolently at his protégé.

"Well, when you're right, you're right, but take a look at this while we wait for whatever lesson Mr. Peter is giving to end. My guess is it isn't horseback riding or bowling." He winked and slid a report of the previous night's crime scene, including a list of fingerprints and their locations on the Bentley, across the desk.

Teresa scanned the letter, then went back and made checkmarks next to a few names and looked up at her part-ner with a furrowed brow.

"What the heck; did he throw parties in that car? There have to be twenty-plus fingerprints here."

Sherlock nodded. "So, what does that tell you?"

Teresa stroked her chin and patted her stomach.

"Hmm... well... Sherlock, I would surmise that he lent the car out often, and perhaps he has another car and was generous to a fault and good-looking to boot."

Sherlock snorted.

"Well, you already knew he was drop-dead handsome, but you nailed it on the other points. I'm guessing he had more than two cars, and he indeed was generous. As the manager at the Bellagio said, the man had many friends, and even though he was a successful poker player, most of them are not. So, he lent his car or cars out to folks if they needed them."

Teresa looked at the list.

"Peter O'Brien's name is here, but that makes sense. But on the other hand, why would he need to be fingerprinted?"

"Look at the footnotes. Our Mr. Peter is a retired Marine. Served in our President Bush's little excursion into Kuwait. No mention of him being gay, though."

Teresa looked up. "Here is a convicted felon that served time in San Quentin. His name is Demetrio Ilhora Quitera, nicknamed DQ, and it says he is Mexican and an albino."

She squinted her eyes and pursed her lips in thought.

"I don't think I have met an albino Mexican."

At that moment, the phone rang, and Sherlock quickly grabbed it.

"Detective Samuel Watson here."

"Hello, hello, this is Peter O'Brien, and tell me this isn't some damn joke. David was always a prankster, and I wouldn't put it past him to set me up like this."

Sherlock hit the speaker button so Teresa could listen in, her notepad in hand.

"No, sir, I wish I could tell you it was a gag, but it most positively is not. I saw your friend... or your fiancé... last night, and he was definitely dead. And I am so sorry for that; from what I have heard about him, sounds like he was a nice guy, generous to a fault."

And he winked at Teresa.

"Oh my God, he was, and to people he didn't even know well."

There was a pause.

"Yes ma'am, I will be right with you. Ah... Detective... I'm sorry; we are shorthanded here, and I need to save my vacation for the funeral. With David gone, I'm living from paycheck to paycheck."

And he hesitated.

"Is there any chance you can come to Las Vegas?"

"Well, I don't know. Tell me why I should."

"Because I have lots to tell you, and in-person is best. I really don't know if you are who you say you are."

Peter hesitated again.

"Do you play golf, Detective?"

It was Sherlock's turn to hesitate.

"I did, but my dear departed wife objected to six hours at the course and the nineteenth hole and booze after it. But I loved the game once."

"Well, there you go. I'm an assistant pro at the Las Vegas Country Club, and I can slide you in about three o'clock Saturday. Just you and me playing, and I'll say I'm giving you a lesson. Most folks don't want to play in the afternoon heat this time of year."

"Well, I don't know."

Teresa nodded affirmatively and whispered, "Just do it!" She added, "No drinking!"

Sherlock smiled a mellow little smile and reversed course.

"You know, Peter, that sounds wonderful. I've never had a lesson; maybe I can learn a thing or two from you. "

"Excellent, then we can chat all you want. I know a couple of members that will say you are their guest. And maybe you will pick up a pointer or two. After all, this is what I do for a living. Be here at, say, two-thirty, and we will chat about David."

Peter paused once again.

"Bring some identification and sunscreen."

And he was gone.

• • • • • • • • • • • •

Sherlock stroked his chin.

"Boy, I'm not sure I should go. Maybe you should go, Teresa, and I'll follow up with Ms. Ruthie."

Teresa laughed.

"I know you really want to go. Yeah, me golfing, now that is a hoot. I've never golfed a day in my life and have no desire to, all that work to put a little ball in a cup and for what? Most golfers that I've met are borderline schizophrenics."

She laughed again. "And yes, that includes you," she beamed at her mentor. "But it takes one to know one."

And she blew him a kiss. "That's why the captain paired us together."

Sherlock scratched the top of his head and frowned, then grinned.

"Well, I'm not so sure about that, but I would love to take up golf again, and that is a fantastic course, and hell, I get a lesson thrown in to boot. All while earning my salary—and no, I won't drink, at least not until we've finished, Mother!"

He snatched the fingerprint list off the desk.

"But that is tomorrow, and time's a-wastin'. Let's head over to Ms. Ruthie's mini-mansion and break the news to her. The officers offered to do it last night, but I told them we would do it this morning."

He looked at his watch.

"Or I guess afternoon; it's time for lunch already, and after that schizo comment, you can buy me lunch."

And he chuckled.

"Oh, pregnant one."

•••••••••••

After consuming an In-N-Out double burger and a large order of fries, the detectives, full and content, rang the doorbell to the Rockefeller mansion. The door was opened by Maria this time, outfitted not in the old-fashioned maid's uniform that she'd worn on the last visit, but in long pants and a long-sleeved shirt, with a bright red kerchief tied around her head. Standing behind her was a tall, gaunt young lady who was dressed the same. Maria nodded at the detectives and motioned for them to come in.

"Ms. Rockefeller is outside on the patio. Let me take you to her." She paused and pointed at the other woman. "This is my granddaughter; she helps me clean the house occasionally. It's really too big for me to do it all by myself," she said with a grimace.

She turned to her granddaughter.

"This is Detective Watson and… um… Detective Teresa?"

She turned back to the detectives.

"My granddaughter, Catalina Esma Balderas."

And the granddaughter simply nodded and looked away, her bloodshot eyes darting back and forth as if looking for a way to escape.

Maria led the way to the patio, where Ruth was lounging in a shady spot, underneath an overhead fan that was cranked on high. She had a pitcher on the side table next to her, and she simply waved the detectives to the patio chairs, not bothering to stand up.

"Well, long time no see, detectives—are you back to have a drink with me? I'm afraid you missed the Bloody Marys from this morning. Gin and tonic is my afternoon drink of choice. Would you like one, Detective Watson? Or I could have Maria fetch you a Maker's Mark."

She turned to Teresa, whose extra-large T-shirt was clinging to her body as a result of the humidity, her belly button looking as large as a moon crater.

"But none for our prego; Maria, fetch her a bottle of cold water."

Maria nearly curtsied, and Sherlock held up two fingers, indicating he would like a bottle of water as well.

Sherlock sat next to Ruth.

"What are you looking at, ma'am?"

"It's Ms. Rockefeller, not ma'am, Detective, and you know it. And these are the stamps that were being appraised. They were delivered yesterday afternoon, and the appraiser said my soon-to-be ex-husband was coming home to look at them. But it's just like him to not show up, and so I took it upon myself to open it and reacquaint myself with them. My God, they are something to behold."

She pointed at an uncanceled stamp that looked older than Methuselah.

"This one is supposed to be worth over a quarter-million dollars. Imagine that for a freakin' stamp. Go figure," she said, irreverently slamming the book closed.

"But they are my husband's, and my prenup says I don't get any of these lickables."

And she smirked.

"So, I'm going to put them back into our safe and not think about them again."

She took a swig of her gin and tonic as Maria appeared from nowhere and handed the detectives bottles of cold water. Maria motioned at the stamp collection. "Would you like me to put them in the den, Ms. Rockefeller? This heat and humidity can't be good for them."

"Yes, please, Maria, that would be good, and is your granddaughter here to help you clean?"

"Yes, ma'am, she is, and if you don't need anything else, I am going to join her upstairs."

Ruth looked at her. "Is that goddamn albino ex-con with her?"

"No, ma'am, you told me not to bring him back here again."

"Damn right, and you should throw him out of your house as well. Is he still living with you and your granddaughter?"

Maria nodded meekly. "Yes, ma'am. He doesn't have a place to live, and my granddaughter is in love with him."

She shrugged and put her arms out at her sides as if to say, what's a grandma to do?

Ruth snorted and glanced at the half-full pitcher of gin and tonic.

"Well, he's not my problem."

And she hesitated.

"I can make another pitcher of gin and tonic if need be, so go look after your granddaughter and make sure she doesn't steal anything... again."

Maria frowned and quickly left, and Sherlock leaned forward.

"She steals things, does she?"

Ruth sipped and smirked.

"Oh yes, that girl is a train wreck. Has a nasty drug habit to feed, and things started to disappear around here. Always

David's things; she knew better than to touch any of my things, or she'd be in jail. No, she took things that she could easily hock, and my husband looked the other way. Hell, he even let her and her God-awful boyfriend, who just got out of prison, use his car for a couple of weeks. What a flaming idiot. He is generous to a fault and thinks everyone deserves a second chance."

And she sipped and laughed nastily.

Sherlock pursed his lips and opened his bottle of water.

"Would this be his Bentley?"

It was Ruth's turn to lean forward.

"How do you know about his Bentley?"

"Well, after all, I am a detective."

He grinned at Ruth and winked at Teresa.

"Would this ex-con boyfriend happen to be Demetrio Il-hora Quitera?"

Ruth set her glass down on the table with a thud.

"How the hell would you know that? And don't give me bullshit about being a detective."

Sherlock chuckled quietly. "Well, his fingerprints were in Davidson's Bentley."

Ruth picked up the pitcher, filled up her glass, and took a hefty gulp.

"How the hell would you know that? The Bentley is in the garage with his other toys."

Sherlock took a cold swig from his water bottle.

"No ma'am, the Bentley is in police custody, as is Davidson."

Ruth started to take a sip of her cocktail but stopped.

"Are you kidding me? What did he do, get busted in a prostitution sting operation?"

She laughed and then took a long drink of her gin and tonic.

"Now that wouldn't surprise me, that god-damned idiot."

Sherlock capped his bottle and sighed wearily.

"No ma'am, your husband was killed last night, and we found his body in the trunk of his Bentley."

Ruth dropped her glass and it shattered, littering the patio's stone surface.

"Oh my God, that can't be right. I mean, he was an idiot but didn't have an enemy in the world. Except maybe me?"

Sherlock leaned forward again and merely said, "Exactly."

•••••••••••••

Teresa stood up, saying, "I'll fetch Maria."

She waddled her way into the house, up the stairs, and past a bedroom and a bathroom. Glancing into the den, she saw that the safe was still open and the books of stamps lay on the desk. She paused, then entered the den, flipped open the stamp collection, and looked at the most valuable stamp.

Teresa shook her head; it seemed no different than the other stamps as far as she could tell, so she took out her phone and took a picture of it just to show her fiancé. She closed the book, looked up at the ceiling, and sucked in her breath. The new smoke alarm was gone, and the old one was back.

"What the hell?" she mumbled to herself.

Just then, Maria stuck her head in the doorway. "Ms. Detective Teresa, are you looking for me?"

Teresa turned toward her.

"Yes, I am. Ms. Rockefeller dropped her glass on the patio and needs you to clean it up."

She paused.

"And as long as I'm up here, I'd like to chat with your granddaughter."

Maria shrugged. "She was here in the den cleaning, but when I brought the stamps up and put them on the desk, she just left, saying she wasn't feeling well, and now I need to clean by myself."

She sighed, turned, and left, scooting down the stairs. Teresa looked at the stamp book and the smoke alarm, and a dark smile came to her face. She moved over to the corner where the now-missing smoke alarm was and looked at the open safe. She then closed the safe and moved back to the corner. Standing on her tiptoes, she tried to envision what a camera in that location would have seen. If the smoke alarm were equipped with Wi-Fi and a camera, and if the camera were positioned just right, then anyone opening the safe could be filmed, capturing the combination. And soon, the stamps would be back in the safe and ready for another burglary attempt.

Teresa carefully made her way down the stairs and back to the patio. Maria was just finishing cleaning up the glass, and Ruth was finishing the last of her gin and tonic with a half-smile on her face and no tears at all.

"Exactly when did this happen, Detective?"

Sherlock nodded. "Yesterday, probably last night. We haven't nailed down the exact time yet. But you don't seem too broken up about it. I mean, he was your husband."

Ruth snorted.

"Oh, for Christ sakes, only in name. Hell, we had never even slept together; he was my beard. Do you know what a beard is, Detective?"

"Oh indeed, I do; I am, after all, a detective," he said with a spiteful sneer.

"So, tell me how he died."

Sherlock looked at Teresa, who shrugged, as if to say, she is going to find out sooner or later.

Sherlock nodded and looked Ruth straight in the eyes.

"He was found in the Bentley, shot in the chest."

Ruth's eyes widened.

"Oh my God, that's terrible. That's just awful," she said, and a lone tear made its way down her face.

"Can you tell me what you were doing yesterday and last night, ma'am?"

Ruth looked up.

"Ah... I guess I'm the prime suspect, aren't I?" She giggled. "Well, that makes sense. And yes, I did it, you bet, I shot the man and enjoyed doing it. It served him right for being such an idiot."

And Sherlock shook his head and chuckled softly.

"Well, there we have it—case closed," he said, winking at Teresa.

"So, Ms. Rockefeller, what was your motive? You were about to be divorced, had your life all planned out with Mary Sweeney, and hell, you had never even consummated your marriage. So, what was your motivation?"

"Oh, I don't know—I just felt like doing it, you know, kind of a lark just to see how it felt. Haven't you ever wondered how it would feel to kill someone, Detective?"

Sherlock leaned back. "Oh, I have." And he paused. "I have killed people in the line of duty, and believe me, it stays with you forever. Still have nightmares about it. But that's neither here nor there."

And he took a deep breath.

"So, tell me, Ms. Rockefeller, tell me how this happened. Where did you shoot him? Was he in the driver's seat or passenger seat? How many times did you shoot him?"

Ruth paused.

"Well, in the driver's seat. Davidson always insisted on driving. He loved all his cars, and I shot him right through the heart just like on television. Just once, and he was dead in a second."

Sherlock stood up.

"Well, ma'am, that's bullshit, and I know it, and I'm guessing you have a watertight alibi, and you're going to play with us just to see how far we would take this."

He inhaled deeply again.

"You know, this is not my first rodeo, and maybe you did kill him, and maybe you didn't, but my gut tells me you didn't. But that's just one man's opinion; maybe the DA will disagree with me. But if I were you, I'd get an attorney, and not your divorce attorney, and make sure nothing happens to your alibi. I don't think you would do well in lockup, even for a day."

And he smirked, turning to leave.

"No Bloody Marys for breakfast there."

• • • • • • • • • • • •

Sherlock and Teresa had ridden together to the Rockefeller mansion, and they stopped for dinner at Chick-fil-A on their way back to the police station. Teresa filled Sherlock in on her suspicions about the disappearing smoke alarm and camera.

"So, you think that Maria's granddaughter and her ex-con boyfriend robbed the Rockefellers the first time, but the real goal was the stamp collection?" he asked.

Teresa nodded, her mouth full of chicken.

Sherlock continued, "I think you're right, and maybe, just maybe, Mr. Rockefeller surprised them the first time, and they shot him.

Teresa took a sip of her cola.

"That's exactly what I'm thinking. And you were so right—Ms. Ruthie was not involved."

Sherlock nodded.

"I'd say the probability was remote. Hell, if she'd stumbled on them, she probably would have shot them. Sounds like she has thought about killing someone before."

"I think she is not only an alcoholic but also a little crazy," Teresa said, popping a french fry into her mouth.

Sherlock chuckled.

"Yeah, you may be right, but that's neither here nor there. We need to think about setting up a trap for our burglars to catch them in the act and then tie them to Davidson's murder. But damn it, I'm headed to Las Vegas."

Teresa snatched a french fry from Sherlock's bag.

"How about if we put a squad or two outside the mansion? After all, she is a suspect in a murder. We can wait until you get back and then pull it off. Maybe even have an officer in the house if they take the bait?"

Sherlock fist-bumped Teresa with a sinful smirk on his face.

"That's why you make the big bucks!"

And Teresa snorted.

"Yeah, right."

• • • • • • • • • • • •

Sam had his clubs, a newly shined pair of white golf cleats, and an unopened bottle of sunscreen in the trunk. He actually enjoyed the drive from Los Angles to Las Vegas. It gave him time to think.

Sam thought about the last few days, he believing that he was close to breaking the case open, as long as DQ took the bait. Sherlock now felt pretty sure that DQ had killed Davidson.

Maybe.

As he continued to drive, random thoughts crossed his mind, and the detective laughed at his nickname. His father, a pediatrician who was in fact named Doctor Watson and a huge fan of the Sherlock Holmes stories, gave it to him. And the moniker stuck.

The fact that Sam turned out to be a detective and not a doctor did not sit well with his father, however. It was okay to read about detectives in a book, but the real Doctor Watson despised any kind of gun and detested the thought of his son carrying one on a daily basis. Furthermore, Sam actually killing a man in the line of duty nearly severed their relationship. But God bless Rox, Sam's dearly departed wife, who smoothed over the rift. She pointed out to the doctor that not only was his other favorite character the gun-toting James Bond, but also that he had seen every Bond movie at least three times. She pointed out that Bond's image revolved around guns and women, and with that, Sam's father relented.

Sam pulled into the Las Vegas Country Club with anticipation. It was his first time golfing after many years, and he wondered how he would do on the course.

He followed the signs to the clubhouse, pulled into a visitor's parking spot, and was impressed when a golf cart pulled in right behind him, then another. A smiling, casually-dressed young man who was obviously associated with the golf course was in one of the carts. He wore khaki shorts, a white golf shirt with a collar, and bright white tennis shoes that looked like they came straight out of the shoebox.

The man in the other cart was not smiling. He was dressed in khakis as well, but wore long pants instead of shorts. He also wore a brown long-sleeved shirt. In addition to a badge on his chest, he wore a belt around his waist that held what appeared to be mace, a flashlight, and a nasty-looking stun gun. His tan head was carefully shaved, and he sported a neatly-trimmed salt-and-pepper goatee.

Sherlock popped the trunk from inside the car, emerging with a smile and holding his detective shield in front of him.

"I'm here looking for Mr. Peter O'Brien."

The security officer relaxed and smiled.

"Yes, sir, absolutely, sir. How can I be of assistance... sir?"

Sherlock chuckled quietly.

"Well, if you give golf lessons, then maybe you should tag along, but you may want to put on some shorts and a T-shirt," he said, looking up at the mid-afternoon sun. The man guffawed, and then his face lit up.

"Hey, aren't you Samuel Watson? By God, you are! Right here in our parking lot. I'll be damned. Detective Samuel Watson, alias Sherlock."

He paused, shaking his head in wonderment.

"I am Richard Washburn, Officer Sergeant Washburn, Hollywood division… retired."

Sherlock grinned and moved toward the golf cart, holding out his hand.

"Burnsey, my God, I didn't recognize you. What's with the shaved head and the goatee? And my God, the last time I saw you, you were as pale as Casper the ghost."

Burnsey shook the detective's hand and stroked his goatee with pleasure.

"Well, you know Captain Miller—no facial hair, shine your shoes every day, and no swearing… goddamn it."

And he laughed.

Burnsey looked at the young man in the other cart.

"Taylor, please look after this man; he is a legend in Los Angeles. The best clearance rating by far in the department's history, and I'm guessing he is here to talk with Peter about Mr. Rockefeller."

At that, Taylor slid into action, taking the car keys from the famous detective and pulling Sherlock's clubs out of the trunk, along with the shiny white pair of golf shoes.

And Burnsey laughed again.

"I guess you can't teach an old dog new tricks," he said, pointing to the shined shoes. He motioned to Sam to climb into his cart, then nodded at Taylor. "I'll deliver him to Mr. O'Brien, and you get them set up." Taylor merely nodded as Sherlock climbed into the cart and Burnsey patted him on his leg.

"Come on, we'll find Peter for you," he said, glancing up at the cloudless sky and sniffing. "I hope you get your round in—rain is headed this way."

Sherlock looked up at the still blue sky. "Really? It doesn't look like rain to me. Do you have some old wound that alerts you before it rains?"

Burnsey laughed again and held out his smartphone.

"Heck no, the weather app says we'll get wind and a thunderstorm about supper time."

Then he sped off, with Sherlock holding on for dear life.

Clutching his sunscreen.

••••••••••••

Major Peter O'Brien looked about as straight as anyone Sherlock had ever seen. He looked like Joe Palooka from the bubble gum cards. He was nearly six foot six and stood ramrod straight. He was wearing what Sherlock now guessed was the country club's uniform: khaki shorts and a white collared shirt. However, unlike the others, his shirt was embroidered with his first name. He greeted the detective warmly, and as Sherlock held up his shield, Peter waved it away.

"No need, detective; I looked you up on the Internet. Turns out you are quite the hero in LA.—breaking up a bank robbery single-handedly and shooting the robbers that were armed with assault weapons. Hell, we could have used your skills in Afghanistan!"

Sherlock grimaced. "Well, I guess I was in the wrong place at the right time."

"Sounds like you were in the right place at the right time." He looked at the detective, who was dressed in long pants.

"Let's get you a pair of shorts and head out. We are on the first tee in twenty minutes. I hope you brought your credit card with you; I'm paying for the lessons, but the shorts are on you."

"Not a problem, and I can certainly pay for my lessons and the round."

Peter twitched out a quiet laugh.

"Well, I lied—I get a few free lessons for prospective members, so it really doesn't cost me anything. But you can buy drinks and dinner after."

"You're on."

•••••••••••••

Sherlock, clad in his new shorts, pulled out his driver, put the tee in the neatly trimmed ground, and placed the brand-new, shiny golf ball on top. He stood up and took a deep breath. Looking out at the green, shimmering fairway, he wondered if this was a good idea after all. Peter might be a suspect in a murder investigation, but making a fool of himself in front of a suspect was not his normal procedure. He took another deep breath, hit the ball as hard as he could, and watched as it sailed nearly three hundred yards and then sliced into the trees.

"Son of a gun," said Sherlock.

Peter stepped up behind him and put his foot on the outside of the detective's.

"Move your foot over just a bit." Then, stepping around Sherlock, he put his own ball on the tee. "Okay, now grip your club." Peter pursed his lips and moved the detective's club a half-inch to the right.

"Now try it again."

And he did, and the ball shot straight down the fairway two hundred and fifty yards, landing smack-dab in the middle. The golfers made their way through the first nine holes, with the detective picking up pointers at each of them.

Major Peter O'Brien nearly wept as he talked about Davidson.

"He was one special man, Detective, and I've met my share of good men in the service. He was one of the most kind, forgiving, and generous men that have ever walked the earth," Peter said, as he wiped away a tear.

"And he had a talent, a God-given talent."

He paused and chuckled softly.

"That's if God likes poker. The man had found his niche in life, and I'll tell you, if he had been a golfer and not a poker player, with that talent, he could have gone head-to-head with some of the greatest."

And the major chuckled again in between tears.

"But he hated golf, thought it was a waste of time, and he was right—unless you are a top-tier player; then you can make a bundle. The rest of us are condemned to being club pros. He played with me on occasion just to humor me, but he made it through four or five holes and then just drove the cart. But as I said, he was a gifted poker player, maybe one of the best of all time."

Sherlock looked over at him.

"Then why haven't I heard of him? I watch the poker championship, and I know some of the best players, like Phil Hellmuth, but I've never heard of Davidson Rockefeller."

Peter shrugged.

"That's because he didn't play in those tournaments. Well, he did when they were new and the price to enter was minimal, but later, when they wanted an arm and a leg and your firstborn for an entry fee, he didn't even bother. What you don't know is that the world's best players come to town to play, and they don't just pack up and leave when they lose. Most of them stick around to watch the final table and bet on the winners. And in the meantime, until the final table, what do you think they do?"

Sherlock hit a three-wood on a par three that landed six feet from the hole, and Peter nodded with approval.

Sherlock poked the club at his playing partner.

"Well, I'm guessing they play poker, and I'm also guessing they played with the late Mr. Rockefeller?"

Peter made his shot, and it landed in a sand trap. He grimaced.

"Exactly, and he made more money in those games than everyone but the two finalists at the final table. Hell, at the end, he was making nearly one million dollars during tournament week, and he played all year round."

The men got in the cart and drove up the path next to the green.

Sherlock waited as Peter dug his cleats into the sand and applauded as the ball lipped the hole and spun away.

"Nice shot. So, you are telling me that Mr. Rockefeller was pretty darn wealthy."

"Oh, hell yes."

And the Marine actually giggled.

"Not as wealthy as he might have been if he wasn't so generous. My God, he probably gave more than a million dollars away. He called them loans, but he knew he would never get the money back. He would loan ten thousand dollars to a man he had cleaned out as long as he left town for a while and played somewhere else. But he always said it was how much good you did for others and not how much money you died with."

Peter wiped away another tear and then sunk his putt.

"Not that he didn't spend money on himself; he loved cars, but he lent them out willy-nilly. He was the most generous man I ever met, and I'm going to miss him. He was the love of my life, and we were going to get married once he filed for a divorce and moved to L.A., into that mini-mansion."

Peter turned his head and wept openly.

Sherlock dug into his golf bag and came up with a small travel bag of tissues. He handed it to Peter, who blew his nose and wiped his bloodshot eyes.

"I'm sorry about that, Detective. Not a manly Marine thing to do, especially on the golf course."

Peter offered the tissue pack back to Sherlock, but Sherlock put up his hand.

"No, you keep 'em, and as for crying about the love of your life, I've been there and done that. I think I cried for three weeks after my wife passed."

Peter dabbed at his eye.

"So, tell me, Detective, how is his quote-un-quote wife taking this?"

The detective paused, not wanting to share too much. After all, Peter was a suspect in the murder... or was he? Sherlock looked at the decorated Marine and made a judgment, mentally crossing him off the suspect list. If Peter did kill his fiancé, then he had missed his calling as well—as an actor.

"Well, she was upset but not overly so, I guess. She figured out pretty quickly that she was going to be a prime suspect, and she even toyed with us and initially said that she did indeed kill him."

Peter smirked and snorted.

"Now that sounds like Ruthie. The woman is mentally ill and loves to toy with people, and you, Detective, would be a prime target. Did you know she is bipolar and an alcoholic as well? She heads to Palm Springs to dry out and get treated by a psychiatrist who graduated from Stanford. I forget her name, but she is one of the leaders in treating people who are bipolar."

Sherlock pulled his driver out of his bag.

"Would that be Mary Sweeney?"

Peter pointed his club at the detective.

"That's it, Mary Sweeney—you must be a detective!"

The detective chuckled.

"Well, they call me Sherlock, so I guess I might be—but tell me about this Ms. Sweeney."

Peter nodded as he teed up the ball and got into a comfortable hitting position. He took a shallow breath and hit the ball too straight and nearly to the moon.

"Well, I don't know much about her, only what David told me, but it's not Ms.; it's Mrs. Sweeney, and she is married to an economics professor, William K. Sweeney, who is famous in his own right. David said they were old-fashioned Catholics and had at least nine children."

The detective settled in and emulated his playing partner, taking a shallow breath this time and hitting the ball down the middle of the fairway—just not to the moon.

"That's interesting; Ms. Rockefeller said Mary Sweeney was gay and the love of her life, and that they were going to get married once she filed for divorce."

Peter blew his nose again and looked over at Sherlock.

"Oh, for Christ sake, that's nonsense."

And he paused.

"But not unlike Ruthie. She may believe it at some level, but Mary Sweeney is definitely not openly gay."

And he paused again.

"But Ruthie is as gay as Ellen DeGeneres, and better looking to boot. She is built like a stripper, and in fact she is... at least on amateur nights. She loves it, and most of her friends are cocaine-snorting hardcore strippers and gay or bisexual as well. David told me they have amateur night at the club in the middle of the week, and she stays out late and parties with her stripper pals until the wee hours of the morning."

Sherlock hit an eight iron, slicing it into the woods. Peter grimaced.

"Tough to think too much on the course and play well, isn't it?"

Sherlock mumbled to himself, "Well, that explains the iron-clad alibi she wouldn't share with us."

Peter hit his shot just short of the green on the par five.

"What did you say, Detective?"

Sherlock pursed his lips as a thunderclap sounded in the distance.

"I said, this case is getting more interesting by the moment."

•••••••••••••

The golfers were on the eighteenth green, and Sherlock was about to putt when a strong gust of wind knocked off his HPD cap, causing him to miss the putt by a foot. Peter reached down and picked up the cap as the skies opened and a torrential rain burst from the clouds. The men dashed to the cart and drove headlong to the clubhouse.

Taylor was patiently waiting for them, and as they drove under the overhang, he handed them each a towel. He grinned at the soaked golfers.

"Darn, you almost made it."

Peter toweled off his head of dark curls. "Oh well, we needed the rain, and I guess I don't need a shower now."

Taylor laughed and turned to the detective. "Mr. Watson... I mean, Detective Watson, I bought you a clean shirt, and it's hanging on your locker."

Sherlock looked at the young man with new respect. "Taylor, you didn't need to do that."

"Well, I was talking to Mr. Washburn, and he told me about how famous you are, and I thought maybe you were going to get caught in the rain and... well... I just did it."

Sherlock reached into his wallet and frowned. All he had left was two dollars and his credit cards.

"Son of a gun. Taylor, you don't take American Express, do you?"

Taylor smiled. "No, sir, and I told you, it's a gift from me, and I would be offended if you paid for it."

Sherlock sighed as he put his wallet back into his wet pants.

"Well, thank you very much, Taylor. Tell me, what is your last name?"

Taylor smiled, stood as straight and tall as he could, and proudly said, "Taylor Humphrey Beasley the Third, sir!"

"Well, Taylor Humphrey Beasley, what could I do for you, sir?" replied Sherlock.

Taylor smiled his best smile and pointed at Sherlock's HPD cap.

"I would like to get your autograph on that cap, and maybe a selfie with you. After what Mr. Washburn told me about the exciting life of a detective, I've decided to become one myself."

Sherlock grimaced as Taylor mentioned his profession but said nothing as he signed the cap and put it on Taylor's head before a wet Peter O'Brien took a picture of the young man and the old detective.

Taylor adjusted his new cap and said, "I'll have everything ready for you, Detective, once you finish your dinner."

And he disappeared.

•••••••••••••

The golfers changed into some dry clothes and sat down for dinner in a small restaurant next to the nearly deserted men's locker room. Peter ordered a Heineken on tap, and Sherlock thought long and hard about it but ordered an Arnie Palmer instead. After all, he was at a famous golf course, and he intended to drive back to Los Angeles tonight, rain or no rain. Peter recommended the meatloaf, which was, in fact, delicious.

No one spoke until the meal ended, but then Peter looked over at his new friend, Sherlock.

"There are a few things that you still need to know, Samuel."

Sherlock nodded, sipping his Arnie Palmer and wishing he were sipping draught Heineken.

"Okay, tell me." And he held up his hand. "Wait! You are going to tell me that I should give up golf forever and take up badminton?"

Peter laughed.

"No, not at all, and for the second nine you were incredible. I know we were not keeping score, but I do, in my head, automatically. And do you know what you shot on the second nine?"

Sherlock shook his head. "I don't know, fifty or fifty-five?"

Peter rolled his eyes.

"Oh, not at all—you shot forty, and if that gust of wind wouldn't have knocked your cap off, you would have shot a thirty-nine. A freakin' thirty-nine, Mr. Sherlock. Hell, that's better than ninety-five percent of the members here. I have got to tell you, you are a natural. Hell, if you were twenty years younger, with a year's worth of practice, you might qualify for the tour."

Sherlock smirked. "Don't bullshit an old man, Mr. Marine."

"Oh no, I'm not bullshitting you at all. I got no dog in this hunt. But that's really neither here nor there. What I really want to tell you is this: David and I were in fact going to get married, and he was instigating the divorce, not Ruth. We were in fact going to leave Las Vegas and move into the mini-mansion. What you don't know about me is that I am an orphan, and David and I were going to open an orphanage. We both love children."

He raised his palms and sighed deeply.

"But being gay does have its setbacks. David was back in town to pick up the stamp collection that his father had left him. He'd had it appraised and was going to offer half the value to Ruth. You see, the mansion was half hers, and he was going to give her up to a million for her share. David said the collection alone was worth up to a million and a half. So that's why he was in Hollywood and not here playing poker."

Peter paused.

"He was also going to be serving divorce papers to his wife, and he wanted to do it in person."

Sherlock took a deep breath, with no golf club in sight.

"Well, that is interesting. So, if Ruth did kill him, she really had no reason to… in hindsight."

Peter furrowed his brow.

"I don't know about that; all I know was that I had landed a job at the Wilshire golf course, as the head pro, and that David would play poker part-time and hire folks to run the orphanage. But now, that is gone, and Ruth gets everything."

The detective interjected. "But she had no way of knowing this ahead of time… right, Peter?"

Peter shrugged and sipped his Heineken.

"I have no idea; you're the detective."

•••••••••••••

Taylor met them at the clubhouse door with an umbrella in hand and his ever-present smile on his face. "Detective Watson, your clubs are in the car," he said, pointing behind him. "I cleaned the clubs and polished your shoes and re-placed a cleat or two. I vacuumed the car and washed it," he added with a shrug. "It wasn't raining then. Sorry about that."

He handed the umbrella to Sherlock.

Peter O'Brien leaned toward Sherlock and whispered in his ear.

"He gave up a nice caddying job this afternoon to tend to you."

Sherlock sighed.

"Taylor, how much do you make caddying?"

Taylor frowned at Peter. "Well, nothing; it's all about the tips, sir."

"And what's the normal tip?"

"Well, forty bucks is average, sir."

Sherlock pulled out his wallet and removed his driver's license, which he had his emergency fifty-dollar bill stashed behind.

He held it in his palm and out of sight.

"Tell me, Taylor, where do you go to school?"

"UCLA," announced Taylor.

"And what are you studying?"

Taylor puffed his chest out. "Pre-med. I'm at the end of my sophomore year."

Sherlock sighed. "And now you want to switch and become a detective?"

Taylor's chest deflated just a bit.

"Yes sir, absolutely."

And Sherlock sighed again.

"Well, why don't you be both?"

Taylor tilted his head, perplexed. "Is that possible, um… sir?"

"Absolutely. Have you ever heard of police medical examiners or forensic pathologists?"

Taylor nodded. "Well, yes, sir, on television."

"Well, for example, forensic pathologists are even more valuable than detectives and make pretty good bucks as well."

Taylor's chest swelled again.

"That sounds very interesting, sir. I think I'll check that out."

Sherlock handed Taylor the fifty-dollar bill.

"Thanks for having my six, Taylor."

Taylor frowned.

"I don't understand."

And it was Sherlock's turn to smile.

"Having my back, and here is fifty bucks for not caddying today. You need to take it, as long as you finish pre-med. Okay?"

Taylor grinned and sucked in his breath.

"Yes sir, absolutely, sir!"

And he saluted Sherlock.

Sherlock returned the salute crisply.

And he winked at Peter O'Brien.

•••••••••••••

With his free umbrella in the back of his car, the detective was hurtling through the rain and the wind as if drilling through the darkness. The country club rules said cell phones were to be left in your locker when on the course, turned off. He had just rested it on the passenger seat as a gust of wind nearly blew him into the next lane. Of course, his phone rang just then. He picked it up and heard a crackly voice.

"Hey Detective, this is Captain Miller. Where the hell are you?"

Sherlock grimaced. He hadn't shared the details of his trip to Vegas with the captain.

"Well, I've been working on the Rockefeller murder," he said truthfully.

"Yeah, well, you haven't been answering your phone, and that's not acceptable."

"Sorry, Cap, the battery was dead, and I just got it re-charged," he lied.

"Yeah, right. But hey, I have good news for you and bad news for you. Which do you want first?"

Sherlock snorted.

"The bad news."

"Okay. I pulled the officers off the Rockefeller place this af-ternoon. Ms. Rockefeller knocked on the window of the squad and said she was leaving for Palm Springs for a week. And get this—she warned the officer not to pee in her front yard but said to feel free to use the bathroom, since she was leaving the door unlocked. She said to guard the place until she got home in a week or two and to help themselves to all the booze they wanted."

The captain chuckled.

"So, I pulled the guys off. It's Mother's Day tomorrow, and these guys are married, and I'm not taking any more angry calls from wives about holidays."

"So, what's the good news?"

"Yeah, the good news is that we now know who killed Mr. Davidson Rockefeller. It was that ex-con albino, Demetrio Quitera—the fuckin' idiot didn't pick up his casing, and we found two excellent prints on them."

The captain paused.

"I guess I have some more bad news: He is in the wind. We went to the address he gave his parole officer, and it belongs to this sweet old Mexican lady, Maria Hernandez. She says she doesn't know him."

The captain's voice broke into static, and the phone went dead.

Sherlock groaned.

•••••••••••••

Teresa was sitting on her three-season porch and enjoying the rain. Her future husband, Will Tecker, was working this Saturday, preparing for a Monday court case defending a group of homeless people who had been told not to sleep on the sidewalks. So, she was alone with her unborn baby, and she relished the time. She had overruled Will on learning the gender of the baby. He'd said they should find out as soon as possible; after all, he was a recent graduate from law school, and he liked closure. Teresa, on the other hand, was a rookie detective, and she liked detecting and very much wanted to be surprised.

And of course, Teresa won that battle, hands down.

Will Tecker was originally from "the Great State of Wisconsin," as he liked to tell his indigent clients. He had graduated from law school at the University of Wisconsin–Madison with honors. His mother and father were so proud of him, their only child. His father had hoped that Will would step up and take over the farm just outside of Colby. But that was not on Will's agenda. The farm was a family farm, but it had grown into one of the largest in the state under the guidance of Will's father, Ed.

Not Edward—just Ed.

What Will did not announce to his clients about Wisconsin was that he really hated cold weather—a lot. So, he picked up and moved to Los Angeles right after graduation, with a promise from his parents that they would visit soon. Which Will thought was bull hockey because they never traveled anywhere, but lo and behold, they did indeed take the trip a year after his graduation.

Unfortunately, they never made it.

Will's mom had never flown and was not about to start, so a week after New Year's Day, they loaded up their brand-new Ford F-150 with a rental trailer attached. It carried some of the things Will had left behind, including his three baseball mitts—a fielder's glove, a catcher's mitt, and a first baseman's glove. Will loved to play baseball, and he was an excellent catcher. Unfortunately, he couldn't pitch worth a darn.

With the trailer behind them, off they went, looking forward to a warm climate on the first vacation they would have since their honeymoon twenty-five years ago. Now Will's mom, Emma, wanted to take their time and see the sights, while Ed looked at all the snow and the fact that it was five above zero and thought they needed to just get pushing forward.

Things were all right until they hit Colorado and the mountains and all the skiers on the roads hurrying through the bitter cold and snow to get their boots on the slopes. It was a Volvo loaded with teenagers still celebrating New Year's that crossed over the center line and sideswiped the Teckers' new pickup truck. Ed had seen the Volvo coming and tried to avoid the collision, but the trailer was his downfall—it swerved back and forth until it finally dropped over the mountain cliff.

Taking the Teckers with it.

The teenagers didn't stop at all, opening another round of beers in silence and hurrying to the slopes. With Will's mom and dad in tow, the trailer and the new Ford plunged nearly a thousand feet into the canyon below.

And exploded.

It was not until two weeks later that one of the teens in the car, at the insistence of her parents, called anonymously and reported the crash.

Then hurried to biology class, satisfied that she had done her duty.

Will Tecker knew his folks were taking their time, and he also knew their route, including the mountains, so when his calls went right to voicemail, he didn't get concerned at all. Two days after the mountain crash, he became worried... very worried. He called the state police in every state on his parents' route and was promised that they would keep an eye out for them. They assured Will that his parents were probably snowed in somewhere, perhaps revisiting their honeymoon. But three more days went by, and then a week, and Will had become frantic—until he got a call from the Colorado State Patrol with the news.

And Will was devastated.

Will Tecker flew to Colorado, identified the bodies, and made arrangements to have them flown to Colby.

His mother's only flight.

He was gracious at the funeral and even sampled the potluck in the church's basement, including the lime Jell-O with shaved carrots and green grapes.

Compliments of his mother's best friend, Betty Sue Gable.

After the funeral, he met with his father's foreman, Caleb Curtis, and his father's lawyer, Emil Ronstadt, and discovered that his father was rich...

Really rich.

What was once a small family farm had expanded into a conglomerate of twelve farms, all owned by Ed and Emma Tecker—and now, apparently, owned by Will. Ed, the wonderful farmer and businessman, and a forward-looking man, had set up a last-to-die insurance policy for himself and Emma. According to Attorney Ronstadt, the policy was intended to cover their estate taxes when Will's parents passed in the very distant future. But there it was, four million in life insurance and the farms as well, which were worth over ten million dollars.

Will hung his head and cried... and cried.

•••••••••••••

Sherlock nearly threw his phone out the window. God was punishing him for telling the captain that the cell battery had died.

That was exactly what had now happened, leaving him stuck halfway between Vegas and Los Angeles in the rain with no way to reach Teresa.

He wondered what she might do when she found out that the Rockefellers' home was unguarded. And then he sighed again. He knew exactly what she would do: she would go herself.

Sherlock punched the accelerator, rain or no rain.

The good news was that the traffic was very light, but the bad news was that the rain and wind were actually picking up. The detective looked into the darkness and saw an ambulance, its light rack flashing into the night, heading back toward Vegas.

And it dawned on him.

He had lights in the grill of his police car. He slowed a bit and turned on the overhead light. He had never used the lights and had no idea what switch operated them. The car was less than two years old, and he drove it because he was the senior detective on the squad. His old unit... his very old unit... had been given to the newest member of the detective squad—Teresa, of course.

There was a lineup of buttons on the dash that he had never touched. He hit the first one, but it didn't seem to do a thing. Then he tried the next one—a sunscreen rose in the back window and Sherlock damn near drove off the road. He flipped the dome switch and the screen retreated to its original position. And he shook his head and mumbled to himself, "I never knew that was there."

He hit the next switch, and voila, the front of the car lit up like the Fourth of July. Sherlock hit the gas as the wind and rain intensified.

And he didn't give a shit.

••••••••••••

Teresa had not budged from the sofa on her three-season porch. The porch was her favorite spot in the tiny home, and she especially loved it when it was raining—and it certainty was now. The evening had grown late, and a hazy nimbostratus rain cloud enveloped the diminutive home. Lightning crackled and sputtered in the darkness, lighting up the sky for an instant. Thunder rumbled and seemed to bounce off the tiny porch roof. The rain poured down in sheets through the darkness, disrupted only by gusts of wind that shook the portico. The downpour blurred the view for Teresa, and she felt as if she were in a cascading waterfall.

Teresa felt a thud in her swollen belly and giggled.

The baby was certainly active and seemed to be wanting out, which was just fine with her. Being pregnant was all right for a few months, but nine months was too long... way too long. Again, she wondered about the gender of the kicking baby. She really didn't care whether it was a boy or a girl. Will wanted a boy, a left-handed boy who would eventually pitch in the major leagues and win the Cy Young award.

Teresa thought just a healthy baby would be just fine.

She sighed lovingly at the thought of her future husband. He had been through so much with the death of his parents and had handled it well, as far as Teresa could tell. She had met him at a Dodgers game. She was sitting right in front of him, and when Robin Yount of the visiting team, the Milwaukee Brewers, hit a home run, Will had leapt up and dumped his big bag of popcorn, extra butter, on her shoulders and back.

And the rest was history.

They knew from that moment on that they were made for each other. Both ceased dating, and each began planning a wedding, just not telling each other. Teresa was in love with Will because of his wonderful values, his sparkling emerald eyes, and his constant devotion. He called her his princess and told her he loved her each morning.

And he did... he really, really did.

He listened patiently on their first date—no baseball or butter involved—about how Teresa had ended up as a citizen of both the U.S. and Mexico. Which was pretty simple: her parents were two of hundreds of thousands that picked the California harvest to feed America. All they needed was a temporary visa, a strong back, and the willingness to work cheaply—very cheaply.

So, Teresa Ramirez was born in the good old USA, outside of Sacramento, California, and as dictated by the Immigration and Nationality Act, she was automatically declared a U.S. citizen. Her parents, Raul and Rosa, did not live in Mexico City as she told most people. Rather, they lived in a tiny town not far from the U.S. border called Zona Norte. Teresa had grown up in the tiny hamlet, at least in the winter. The town had been a supplier of sex workers for Tijuana for decades, but Teresa's baseball scholarship had helped her dodge that particular bullet. However, it recently had been taken over by the smaller of the drug cartels operating out of Tijuana, the Sinale. It was one of the smallest cartels, and by virtue of that, the most ruthless. Her parents hated it and lived in constant fear.

But there was good news.

When Teresa met Will, she had no idea how incredibly wealthy he was. When they went to ball games, which they did on a regular basis, he popped for budget seats. Not until he had knelt down in front of her in their favorite Mexican restaurant, Josie's, with the three guitar players backing him up, and she accepted the most beautiful five-carat ring she'd ever seen, did she learn that he was wealthy—very wealthy. And when she found out, not wanting to be viewed as a gold digger for the rest of her life, she almost canceled the wedding.

Almost.

But now they were committed. One too many margaritas at Josie's and unprotected sex had led to the little one in her belly—the future Cy Young award winner, which Teresa quietly supported, especially if it were her daughter.

She and Will were making her parents very happy by bringing them back to the U.S. with a permanent visa and a path to citizenship, which amazed Teresa. Apparently when you are rich, immigration rules do not apply. And Will, of course, was rich, and a few large contributions to California and Wisconsin senators and congressmen allowed Teresa's parents to jump the line, now proud owners of long-term visas that would result in them becoming Americans.

And Teresa was thrilled.

One summer years before she had met Will, when she was seventeen and old enough to work side-by-side with her parents in the fields, a young Mexican boy had developed a crush on the pretty young Teresa. And one hot August day, he demonstrated his love by drilling her in the chest with an avocado.

Really?

Teresa was none too thrilled. So, she did what every blue-blooded U.S. citizen would do.

She reciprocated.

And she damn near killed him. Apparently, Teresa was a natural in the throwing department, and she'd whacked the young man in his face and chest, then again in his face—all with rock-hard avocados. She hit him at will, and exactly where she intended, which resulted in two things.

She broke the young man's nose as well as his heart, and the entire event was witnessed by Phil Magladrey, the avo-cado field's owner, who was a USC graduate and a fairly good pitcher for the college team in his day.

And he was impressed—very impressed.

So, he pulled her aside the next day with the permission of her parents and assurances that she would get paid. And Teresa got to throw a real baseball—the first she had ever seen. Magladrey pulled out a catcher's mitt, filled up a bucket of balls, and told Teresa to let 'er rip.

And she did. Boy oh boy, did she. And Teresa's baseball career was born. A college education and a full scholarship, too—to USC, of course. And Teresa's life was never the same. She was the ace of the staff from the moment she set foot on the mound, and she was actually a decent hitter—especially if you counted bunts.

And she did.

So, she played ball for the university and studied as hard as any student ever had. After all, her athletic career was going to be short-lived, and she never wanted to pick another avocado in her life.

Eating them, good. Picking them... bad.

She graduated with honors with a degree in criminal justice, vowing to return to Mexico to take on the bad guys. Which, up to this point, she'd never done.

Phil Magladrey gave her an extra-special graduation gift. He paid five thousand dollars for her tuition at the best private police academy in the state, and Teresa's life was set. Her instructor was a gruff man with a kind heart—especially toward women, and he took to her immediately. Which meant he rode her harder than the men and made her do everything twice, and Teresa loved him for it. But the real breakthrough was when a certain guest speaker came to the academy. They had one every other day, but this one... this one was special. His name was Detective Samuel Watson, and his nickname was...

Sherlock!

Sherlock, a soft-spoken man, talked about his love of being a detective. A calling that he said was only for a chosen few but rewarding... very rewarding. He talked about some of the cases he had handled in the Hollywood department, which had combined its robbery and homicide cases, given their limited staff. At the prodding of the class instructor, he even revealed how he had been in his bank at the wrong time and had thwarted a robbery single-handedly, killing all three bank robbers. He added that it was the saddest day of his life, and that it had almost caused him to resign.

He talked about helping victims and volunteering at a homeless shelter. When three of the shelter's patrons had been killed by the volunteer chef, the detective stepped in every other week to cook, alongside with his dear wife Abigail—an excellent cook and the love of his life. At least, that is what the detective announced... with a smile that broke Teresa's heart.

After her graduation, the LAPD offered Teresa a position as a rookie officer. They had bent over backward to get a smart, Hispanic woman into their ranks. And the fact that she was a phenomenon on the pitcher's mound certainty didn't hurt. So, she spent seven years on the streets and rose to the rank of lieutenant. Then, one day she ran into Sherlock—believe it or not, at the Dunkin' Donuts shop.

And he immediately recognized her.

A year and a half later, with some strings having being pulled by Sherlock and the new Captain Miller, Teresa moved from the LAPD to Hollywood as a greener-than-green detective grade one.

And she was thrilled, again.

•••••••••••••

Sherlock was forty miles outside of Los Angeles when he looked at his gas gage and swore. He was damn near out of gas when he pulled into the next service station. He quickly filled his tank and realized that he really needed to pee—thanks to the three Arnie Palmers. So, he went into the gas station and headed for the bathroom in the rear of the building, and, lo and behold, he saw a phone... a real live payphone. And he smirked—then he pushed through the men's room door and peed like a racehorse.

When nature calls, nature calls.

Sherlock paid for the gas and a Snickers bar, got change for the payphone, and checked his messages. There were several from the captain, of course, and one from Peter saying how he'd enjoyed the golf outing—and one tense one from Teresa.

A really tense message.

•••••••••••••

Teresa was absentmindedly patting her stomach as the wind died down, and the rain had settled into a drizzle when her cell phone rang. She picked it up, thinking the call was from her hubby, but a strange number appeared on the screen, and she almost rejected it... almost. And thank God she didn't, because it was Officer Squeaky on the other end, and he was none too happy.

"Hey Tiger, how are they hanging?"

Teresa chuckled to herself. Now that she knew Squeaky was gayer than Freddie Mercury, she cut him some slack.

"Hanging fine, officer. How are yours hanging?"

Squeaky paused, realizing his error.

"I'm sorry about that, Detective; that was out of line."

Teresa chuckled out loud.

"No, that's okay, Officer Bailey; after hauling this baby around for nine months, I wish I had something hanging in front of me so Will could deliver this little one."

Officer Bailey breathed a sigh of relief.

"Say, I don't know if you heard, but the Cap just pulled the guards off the Rockefeller house. Something about the wife heading to Palm Springs and the Cap wanting the guys to be home for Mother's Day."

And Teresa swore like a drunken sailor.

"Whoa, whoa, little lady, it's not the end of the world."

Teresa thought to herself, the hell it isn't.

She focused and replied.

"Hey, thanks for the heads up, Squeaky. I owe you one."

"Hey, you are welcome. I wish I could help out, but I'm on my way to San Diego to celebrate Mother's Day with my mom."

And Teresa crossed him off the help list.

"Hey, not a problem. You have a safe trip."

The officer paused.

"Oh, and happy Mother's Day."

Teresa chuckled.

A little premature, Squeaky, a little premature.

She immediately dialed Sherlock's cell and the call went straight to voicemail.

"Hey partner, I don't know if you heard, but the Rockefeller mini-mansion is unguarded, and Ms. Ruthie is headed to Palm Springs. So, I'm going to head over there and sit on it."

And she stopped.

"If you get this message, come help me out."

• • • • • • • • • • • • •

Sherlock listened to Teresa's message and swore.

"Goddamn it, that is just like her. Son of a bitch."

He hung up the phone and sprinted to the fully fueled car, thinking to himself, son of a Goddamn bitch... what are the chances of the killer burglars showing up tonight?

And he swore again as he punched the accelerator to the floor, his grill light flashing in the rain.

"Pretty damn good if Mr. ex-con albino is still living with Maria. Hell, she has a direct route into all that goes on in that house," he mumbled to himself.

He swore again.

•••••••••••••

Teresa pulled up to the dark mansion, got out of the car, popped her umbrella open, and walked up to the door. She knocked, and then knocked again, and again, harder, and the door moved just a bit. She almost jumped back—the door was open. Teresa looked around her. The dark street was empty. No fools, these neighbors; they knew when to come in out of the rain.

Teresa pushed open the door and yelled out, "Anyone home? Ms. Rockefeller? Ruth? Maria? Hello, hello?"

Silence.

Teresa stroked her chin and patted her belly without knowing she was doing it, and a plan began to formulate in her devious detective mind. She turned and waddled back to her car, shutting it off. She then got back out of the old automobile, grabbing her purse, and was about to slam the door shut when a downpour of rain and frigid wind swept up her back and she shuddered, chilled to the bone. She opened the car door, retrieved her wet umbrella, and struggled to open it in the cold rainy gusts as she tossed her purse onto the seat. The umbrella popped open with a swish as the wind slammed the car door shut. Just then, a car passed her, hitting a puddle and nearly drenching her, and she swore once again.

"Goddamn it!"

As she gave the tail light of the offending automobile the finger, another gust of wind nearly swept the umbrella out of her hand. Then she determinedly marched—or rather, waddled—up to the dark house. She pushed the door open, went inside, and breathed a sigh of relief.

Thank God!

••••••••••••

Catalina and DQ didn't even notice the unmarked police car or Teresa giving them the finger. They were focused on the Rockefellers' mini-mansion as they passed the dark home and headed around the block. They circled two more times before feeling satisfied that the house was unoccupied, then DQ parked right out front and killed the lights.

Catalina leaned down, snorted a line of cocaine from the back of a book, and giggled.

"What the fuck is so funny?" DQ snorted.

She pointed at the book. It was the Holy Bible, and she giggled again.

"My Goddamn grandmother must have half a dozen Bibles. Hell, I think it's the only book she has ever read."

She paused.

"I sure hope she doesn't mind our taking her car."

DQ took the last bite of a gyro sandwich, extra extra garlic, leaned down, and snorted a line for dessert.

"Are you kidding me? She had enough port to float a ship, and I'm thinking she is seeing visions and dreaming about Jesus or Moses or whatever the hell she dreams about."

He stroked his nose, pulled out his handgun, put it behind his belt against his back, and started to get out of the car.

"Hey, are you sure you don't want me to come with you?" Catalina said.

"No freakin' way; you need to stay here and keep watch and have my back. If this is a freakin' trap, call me on my cell and get the hell out of here. I'll find a way to get back to your grandmother's place."

And he dashed toward the door in the rain, still high on cocaine and grasping Maria's house key. He opened the door, not even noticing that it was already unlocked, and slammed it shut behind him with a drug addict's fury.

Teresa, who was upstairs in the den and attempting to dry her hair with a borrowed towel, sat upright in the overstuffed leather chair.

She leaned over and turned off the desk lamp, reaching out for her purse so she could turn on her cell phone's flashlight, and quietly swore again.

"Son of a bitch, it's in the car, along with my gun. Damn it!"

Then, hearing a creak on the stairs, she scooted into a cluttered closet, leaving the towel on the leather chair and the door open just a crack.

DQ crept up the stairs and slowly stuck his head into the den. He reached around the corner, flipped on the overhead light, and grimaced.

He had been in this room before.

And that visit hadn't gone well... not well at all. He had no idea that Davidson was in Los Angeles, and he certainly had no idea he was in the house. Hell, he'd been told the man was playing poker in Las Vegas and chasing male hookers. But just when he got the safe open, sure enough, the man strode into the room armed with nothing but a scowl.

The idiot.

So DQ sat him down in the chair at gunpoint, and Catalina wailed when she realized the safe was empty.

And it was Davidson's turn to giggle—well, not so much giggle as let out a hefty chortle. DQ pointed the gun at him.

"Where the hell is the freakin' jewelry and gold coins, and that stamp collection and the other shit that was supposed to be in here?"

Davidson extended his arms in bewilderment.

"The stamp collection is being appraised, and as for the rest, I'm sure Ruthie drank it up with her stripper friends. Unless she spent it on treatment in Palm Springs?"

He paused.

"And if she did, good for her."

After DQ bundled him up and forced him into the trunk of his precious Bentley at gunpoint, with Catalina following in her grandmother's car, they drove to the world-famous Hollywood sign.

Which DQ thought was a nice touch.

Catalina was all for leaving him unharmed in the trunk, since she knew Davidson well and thought he probably wouldn't even report the potential burglary. After all, they really hadn't stolen a thing. But DQ, fresh out of prison, was having none of it, and he popped open the trunk and shot the poker player—once, twice, three times, until they both lost track.

With a demonic sneer on his face.

•••••••••••••

But this time, with the hidden Teresa peeking out of the closet, there was no Davidson to deal with. DQ moved

quickly to the safe and looked down at the combination tat-
tooed on the inside of his left forearm.

He deftly opened the safe, and voila, the stamp collection
was back in all its glory!

And he giggled once again.

Teresa watched the albino through the cracked closet door.
The man was tiny, with the beginning of a receding hair-
line. His dishwater-blond hair, dyed pink at the ends, was
pulled into a ponytail. His now-wet, dirty T-shirt said "Go
To Hell" on the front and depicted a skull and crossbones
design underneath. He was certainly an albino, and even
from her position across the room, Teresa could tell that he
reeked of garlic.

And she almost sneezed.

Teresa quickly stepped out of the closet, pointed her finger
at DQ as if she were brandishing a pistol, and held out her
badge in front of her.

******

Sherlock pulled up behind Maria's car and stepped out into
the wind and rain with his gun drawn. He crept up to the
car on the street side and was surprised to see Catalina
slumped over the steering wheel with a vacuous smile on
her face, cocaine on her nose and chin, apparently off in
never-never land. The detective thought about calling it in
but knew his cell phone was dead, and his police vehicle
apparently came loaded with everything except a two-way
radio.

Go figure.

So, he left sleeping beauty in the car and dodged his way through the rain to the front door. He turned the knob and entered. The house was dark for the most part, and he paused. He heard voices on the upper level—a whiny voice that he did not recognize, and then a voice that he was all too familiar with, Teresa Ramirez's. She was his partner and best friend, as well as the daughter that he never had.

And his head nearly exploded.

•••••••••••••

"Hold it right there, mister—you are under arrest. Put your hands behind your head."

DQ slowly turned around, holding the precious stamp collection in his greedy little hand, and started to shake with laughter.

"What the hell are you going to do, lady, shoot me with your finger?"

He shifted the book of stamps to his left hand and pulled his handgun from behind his back. The gun was loaded with copper-blunt Hydra-Shok cartridges, 147-grain, developed for the FBI in 1988. The bullets were unique in appearance, short and stocky with a stemmed hollow point.

The bullets were man-stoppers—woman-stoppers—baby-stoppers.

The stinky albino looked at Teresa's swollen belly and pointed the gun directly at her umbilicus, beginning to squeeze the trigger with a grin on his face.

"All right, two for one!"

Teresa took an involuntary step back and slipped on a small puddle of rainwater, vanishing behind the desk. She hit the back of her head on the hardwood floor with a resounding thud. The bullet passed right over her nose, and she swore she could feel the heat.

DQ swore and pointed the gun again.

"Hey asshole, over here!"

DQ turned quickly, his eyes opening wide as saucers as he began to pull the trigger—alas, just a little too late. Sherlock watched DQ drop as if his bones were made of sawdust, his gun falling to the floor, followed by the stamp collection. The man was obviously dead.

And Sherlock groaned—he had killed a man.

Once again.

• • • • • • • • • • • •

Catalina awoke to the sound of gunfire. She looked all around her and recognized the detective's car parked right behind her. She started the car and began to put it into drive—and then she stopped. She heard another shot, put the car in park, took a deep breath, and shut the car off. She opened the door and stepped out into the wind and rain, feeling as if she were in a dream—a nightmare—as the rain soaked her from head to toe.

And she giggled a cocaine giggle.

As if sleepwalking, she headed down the walkway, climbed the steps, and entered the house, leaving the door wide open. She then looked up the stairs and saw the light on in the den. She climbed the stairs and found him, her albino buddy, on the floor in front of the safe, deader than a door-nail. She crumpled to the floor and cradled DQ's head, kissing his forehead, and began to weep, whispering, "Oh my God, they killed you. Oh my God, they killed you."

•••••••••••••

Sherlock called out, "Teresa, are you okay?"

A strained voice came from behind the desk.

"No, I'm not okay. I think my water just broke and... and... holy shit, the little one is coming! Help me, Samuel, help me."

And Sherlock did just that.

He dropped to the ground behind the desk and without hesitation, stripped Teresa's pants and undies off as if he had delivered babies before. He grabbed the wet towel and handed it to Teresa to squeeze.

"Oh yes, the little one is coming out. Can you squeeze, Teresa? Squeeze!"

She tried and tried and tried, but the towel was not doing the trick.

Sherlock looked up at the desk and grabbed what looked like a small globe, which was actually an expensive paperweight—and really, really heavy. Its glass interior held every color of the rainbow, looking like colored lightning strikes.

Appropriate for the storms today, thought Sherlock.

And he quickly handed the paperweight to Teresa.

"Here, squeeze this; squeeze harder," he said, and she took the paperweight and did just that, and sure enough, it worked.

A beautiful little boy slid out after a few minutes of squeezing, and the little guy cried and cried.

•••••••••••••

Catalina kissed the dead man's lips, then she spotted the gun. She reached out and gripped it, and it slid into her hand as if it were made for her. The gun was cool to the touch and obviously a fine weapon, even to her untrained eye. She squinted and shuddered, and she felt the anger and the animus rise from her gut to the back of her throat, which was now coated in bile. She stood up as if rising from the grave, with the gun in her hand. She moved toward the voices behind the desk, unhurried and deliberate, shuffling and zombielike, pushing her way around the elaborate desk.

Sherlock was cradling the newborn in the wet towel and thinking about whether he needed to cut the umbilical cord—totally unaware that Catalina was right behind him.

But Teresa certainly noticed, and she damn well knew that she needed to do something.

Quickly.

As Catalina began to squeeze the trigger, Teresa, the former college pitcher, reared back and threw the best pitch of her life.

Smack-dab into Catalina's forehead.

Catalina's head snapped back, and she collapsed.

And joined her boyfriend in hell.

Sherlock, the baby deliverer, turned and looked over his shoulder as he handed the newborn to his mother, and smiled.

"Nice shot."

He winked at her as he gazed at the beautiful baby boy, all thoughts of what had happened in the den out of his mind.

"So, Mom, what are you going to name him? Will?"

Teresa looked at him with a daughter's affection.

"No, not at all. Will and I decided ahead of time that if it was a boy, his name would be Samuel... Sam for short."

She hesitated and chuckled.

"And maybe with the middle name 'Sherlock,' but we are not totally sure about that!"

They both laughed.

And Sherlock blushed at the compliment of having someone named after him. As he gazed at the mother and child, he glanced at the clock on the wall.

It was nearly one a.m. on Sunday, Mother's Day.

And he gently squeezed Teresa's hand and simply said, "Happy Mother's Day, Tiger."

Epilogue

DQ and Catalina did not end up in Hell together. Catalina spent a few years in purgatory and atoned for her sins. After all, it was DQ who had gotten her hooked on drugs and pushed her into her brief life of crime.

The good Lord took his time—normally a stint in purgatory lasted less than a year, one and a half years max—but the good Lord was on the fence. After all, Catalina had been involved in a murder... kind of. It was the "kind of" that finally let her off the hook. When she finally got to heaven, the Lord handed her a Bible with instructions to read it and not snort cocaine off the cover.

DQ, on the other hand, went straight to Hell. He did not pass Go, and he did not collect $200—or a single valuable stamp, for that matter. Now, the Devil, who actually preferred to be called Satan, since he thought it was statelier, had a separate section for albinos. They were obviously sensitive to sunburn, or any kind of burn, so Satan thought it best for them to get used to the heat gradually. After all, they were here for eternity, and Satan was in no hurry. But just to be fair to the other inmates, the albinos were forced to put together a singing group, or rather, a wailing group, that was required to perform at the Halloween party. DQ actually enjoyed it as much as one could enjoy wailing. He had been awfully good at it on Earth, so he had a head start on most of the other albinos in his group. He was still learning to gnash his teeth... but it was coming right along.

•••••••••••••

Maria Lopez Hernandez and her future were debated in the district attorney's office at length. The senior DA was convinced that she should be charged; after all, she had been feeding information to her granddaughter and DQ, and he thought she was indirectly complicit in Davidson's murder. But it was iffy, to say the least, and they decided not to press charges. After all, she was out of a job at the mansion and living on social security. At least that's what the DA thought. But Maria had in fact landed on her feet, so to speak. Her best friend Benita Unamunsaga Ballesteros had passed away. Benita, nicknamed BUG, of course, had been employed at St. Vincent's Catholic Church as a live-in housekeeper, maid, and keeper of the rectory. And Maria stepped right into her friend's role without missing a beat. Maria's house was sold for a hefty profit, and she developed the habit of hopping on a casino bus full of little old ladies and playing the slots on Saturday nights, making new friends and winning occasionally.

•••••••••••••

Captain Miller abruptly retired from the police force when his parents died within three weeks of one another. As an only child, he was named the sole beneficiary of both of their life insurance policies. The Cap now had all the money he needed for two lifetimes... the problem was, he had no interests outside of his police career and shining his shoes religiously each morning. Now, retired, he shined them all every morning until his wife sent him packing. So, he met a few of his older friends—actually, arms-length acquaintances—at McDonald's for a late breakfast. And it was there that Phil Dunlop, a retired barber, suggested that since the Cap was so freakin' wealthy, why didn't he buy out the fellow that owned all the shoeshine booths at the Los Angeles airport. And by God, that is just what the Cap did.

He even pitched in and shined some shoes himself.

•••••••••••••

Rosa and Raul Ramirez, Teresa's parents, were welcomed with open arms when their visas were awarded. They moved into the basement of Teresa and Will's home until permanent living accommodations could be secured for them. Will loved it because he was working all the time. And Teresa put up with it because she had live-in babysitters. But the problem of housing appeared out of nowhere, and the idea came from Davidson's funeral.

•••••••••••••

Peter O'Brien wept openly at Davidson's funeral, and his newfound friend, Sherlock, comforted him as best he could. After the funeral, Teresa, sans baby (which was with her parents), Will, Sherlock, and Peter were the last to leave the basement of the church. As the mourners got acquainted, Will inquired about Peter's plans for his job in Los Angeles, as well as for the Rockefeller mini-mansion. Peter threw his hands in the air. "I don't know; everything is on hold now. Ruth is putting the mansion up for sale, and I surely don't have the money that David had—that all went to Ruth."

Will looked at Peter.

"What if I told you that I would purchase the mansion for you as long as you operate it as an orphanage?"

And Peter O'Brien wept again.

●●●●●●●●●●●●

Ruth Rockefeller, with her newfound riches, put the mansion up for sale immediately—hell, she'd never liked it anyway. She made an offer and bought up the Bottoms Up strip club. She immediately got rid of the management and moved into the small apartment in the back, running the club herself. It turned out she was pretty good at it. She planned to have a night where she was the featured stripper, and she immediately quit drinking and hired a personal trainer to get in shape.

Cocaine use was a different matter.

●●●●●●●●●●●●

Teresa Garcia Asia Ramirez was promoted to detective level two as a result of her closing both the burglary and the murder, which pissed off most of the rest of the Hollywood police force—so she declined the promotion. Not. She knew damn well she owed most of the quick promotion to her Mexican ancestry, but what she didn't know was that the committee was even more impressed with her accurate throw and the fact that she'd killed Catalina right after giving birth. They even joked about how they might arm the officers with baseball-size paperweights.

Samuel Raul Tecker was a delightful baby and often slept through the night. Thank God. Teresa felt no remorse for pitching Catalina into hell; after all, she'd been defending Sherlock, herself, and more importantly, the future Cy Young award winner.

Her mother and father had accepted Will's offer to move into the Rockefeller mansion and serve as house parents to the orphans. Will and Peter had been busily recruiting professionals to run the orphanage, but someone needed to live there with the little ones permanently, and her parents were the perfect choice. They'd always wanted more than one child.

•••••••••••••

Detective Samuel Watson was thinking about retiring and taking up golf again. And Teresa really hoped he would not actually pull the trigger... so to speak. She had so much to learn, and he was just the detective, friend, and bonus father that could mentor her. After all, he was Sherlock. However, the fact that he had killed another human being was giving him nightmares... again. It was too late to go to medical school and make his father happy, though.

So, he mulled it over and took some much-needed vacation, which he was now spending playing golf. And Peter O'Brien was right, he was pretty darn good—even better than he was before he had quit for his wife. Go figure. He took a few lessons at the Westchester public course where he knew the pro, Sandra. Hell, he took quite a few lessons, and on his good days and her bad days, he was beating her. Which didn't sit well with her. Sherlock made up for it by buying her dinner, and she was grateful. And in fact, she reciprocated, twice. She was ten years younger than Sherlock, and excellent company. She had been on the women's tour and had won four major championships in her time.

What the detective really liked about her was that she was gay. It was just too soon to actually have a real date, with his wife having passed so recently. And Abigail would have loved the fact that he was having an occasional dinner out. With a lesbian.

When Sherlock had mentioned retiring to Teresa, she did not comment, but he knew she didn't much care for the idea. She was, in a lot of respects, still wet behind the ears, promotion or no promotion. So, he was thinking of sticking around for one more year and helping her learn the ropes, and perhaps continuing to take lessons from his new lesbian buddy, and then... possibly... perhaps... trying to qualify for the senior professional golf tour.

Possibly.

Acknowledgements

I would like to start by acknowledging you, the reader. I know that your time is valuable, so I appreciate the time you spend reading this collection of short stories.

I would also like to thank my various editors and manuscript reviewers.

First, I could not have done this without the quick turnaround of Michael Price and all his talented editors at Edit24-7. Second, the additions from John Fox and his organization Book Fox were amazing, especially because "Just Another Morning" was very real to him, as he was in New York on that fateful day. His descriptions of the storm of dust and ash that he encountered as he fled down the New York streets sent chills up my spine. If you like short stories, his book, *I Will Shout Your Name*, is awesome.

Also, my editor and friend Melinda Nelson is simply the best. My buddy, editor, and former bass player Ken Schubert moved other projects aside to help me produce this book in record time, and I'm thankful for his efforts.

Finally, I dedicate this book to Paula—a great editor and proofreader and, most of all, a wonderful wife.

Peace,

EAF

About the Author

E. Alan Fleischauer is a certified financial planner with a master's degree in financial services, specializing in retirement planning. He has written five novels. The first, *Rescued,* is a semifinalist for the 2019 Laramie Award for Best Western. He lives with his wonderful wife Paula in Minnesota.

.

Also by E. Alan Fleischauer

RESCUED
A Murder Mystery Western

HUNTED
An Intriguing Western

KIDNAPPED
A Suspenseful Western

TOMMIES
A Western Detective Series

JUST DIE
A Contemporary Novel

CHARLIE LOU GOES TO THE RODEO
A Children's Picture Book